THE WOLF

THE GRAY WOLF

AND OTHER STORIES

BY

GEORGE MACDONALD

ILLUSTRATED
BY
CRAIG YOE

WM. B. EERDMAN'S PUBLISHING CO.

Copyright © 1980 by Wm. B. Eerdmans Publishing Co.
255 Jefferson Ave. S.E., Grand Rapids, MI 49503

Illustrations Copyright © 1980 by Craig Yoe
174 Portage Drive, Akron, Ohio 44303

CONTENTS

ILLUSTRATIONS

The story-title decoration is based on an anagram George
MacDonald invented from the letters of his name. It was adopted
as a family emblem.

PUBLISHER'S NOTE

" **I**T must be more than thirty years ago that I bought . . . *Phantastes*. A few hours later I knew I had crossed a great frontier. . . . What it actually did to me was to convert, even to baptise, my imagination."

In those words C. S. Lewis, creator of the Narnia Chronicles, reported his discovery of George MacDonald, one of the nineteenth-century innovators of modern fantasy. Thanks in part to Lewis's appreciation—"I regarded him as my master"—MacDonald came to influence not only Lewis himself but that circle of Lewis's friends in Oxford who called themselves the Inklings. Included were Charles Williams and—more famously—J. R. R. Tolkien, who has paid his own tribute to the "power and beauty" of MacDonald's accomplishment.

George MacDonald was born in 1824, five years later than Queen Victoria; he died four years after her, in 1905. His birthplace was Huntly, Aberdeenshire, in Northwest Scotland, and his Scottish background shows through his work, in its kindly but unsentimental astringency and its love of the commonplace, even more clearly than does the Victorian world in which he later moved as a resident of London. In 1840 he entered Kings College at Aberdeen, and ten years later he became clergyman to a chapel at Arundel, a position he left in 1853 to begin what was to be a long career as highly respected writer, lecturer, and preacher. Among his literary friends were Carlyle, Tennyson, William Morris, and Lewis Carroll. In 1872 he travelled on a spectacularly successful lecture tour of the United States, where he was hailed by the popular press and saw such prominent men of letters as Whittier and Emerson.

MacDonald wrote a number of conventional Victorian novels, modestly successful in his own time but of interest now largely as period pieces. It is for his entrancing fantasy that MacDonald is justly revered today by an enthusiastic and growing readership. These fantasy works include the adult "Faerie Romances" *Phantastes* and *Lilith* and three full-length children's classics: *At the Back of the North Wind, The Princess and the Goblin*, and *The Princess and Curdie*.

Much of MacDonald's best fantasy writing, however, is found in his shorter stories, which in his lifetime were published in such collections as *Adela Cathcart* (1864) and *The Gifts of the Child Christ, and Other Tales* (1882). In the present volume and its companion volumes in THE FANTASY STORIES OF GEORGE MACDONALD, editor Glenn Sadler has compiled a complete edition of MacDonald's shorter works, newly illustrated by artists Craig and Janet Yoe.

"I do not write," MacDonald once said, "for children, but for the childlike, whether of five, or fifty, or seventy-five." Here, then, for the childlike of all ages, is a collection of fairy tales and stories certain to delight both confirmed MacDonald readers and those about to meet him for the first time.

THE GRAY WOLF

ONE evening-twilight in spring, a young English student, who had wandered northwards as far as the outlying fragments of Scotland called the Orkney and Shetland islands, found himself on a small island of the latter group, caught in a storm of wind and hail, which had come on suddenly. It was in vain to look about for any shelter; for not only did the storm entirely obscure the landscape, but there was nothing around him save a desert moss.

At length, however, as he walked on for mere walking's sake, he found himself on the verge of a cliff, and saw, over the brow of it, a few feet below him, a ledge of rock, where he might find some shelter from the blast, which blew from behind. Letting himself down by his hands, he alighted upon something that crunched beneath his tread, and found the bones of many small animals scattered about in front of a little cave in the rock, offering the refuge he sought. He went in, and sat upon a stone. The storm increased in violence, and as the darkness grew he became uneasy, for he did not relish the thought of spending the night in the cave. He had parted from his companions on the opposite side of the island, and it added to his uneasiness that they must be full of apprehension about him. At last there came a lull in the storm, and the same instant he heard a footfall, stealthy and light

Reprinted from *Works of Fancy and Imagination* (1871).

as that of a wild beast, upon the bones at the mouth of the cave. He started up in some fear, though the least thought might have satisfied him that there could be no very dangerous animals upon the island. Before he had time to think, however, the face of a woman appeared in the opening. Eagerly the wanderer spoke. She started at the sound of his voice. He could not see her well, because she was turned towards the darkness of the cave.

"Will you tell me how to find my way across the moor to Shielness?" he asked.

"You cannot find it to-night," she answered, in a sweet tone, and with a smile that bewitched him, revealing the whitest of teeth.

"What am I to do then?" he asked.

"My mother will give you shelter, but that is all she has to offer."

"And that is far more than I expected a minute ago," he replied. "I shall be most grateful."

She turned in silence and left the cave. The youth followed.

She was barefooted, and her pretty brown feet went catlike over the sharp stones, as she led the way down a rocky path to the shore. Her garments were scanty and torn, and her hair blew tangled in the wind. She seemed about five and twenty, lithe and small. Her long fingers kept clutching and pulling nervously at her skirts as she went. Her face was very gray in complexion, and very worn, but delicately formed, and smooth-skinned. Her thin nostrils were tremulous as eyelids, and her lips, whose curves were faultless, had no colour to give sign of indwelling blood. What her eyes were like he could not see, for she had never lifted the delicate films of her eyelids.

At the foot of the cliff they came upon a little hut leaning against it, and having for its inner apartment a natural hollow within it. Smoke was spreading over the face of the rock, and the grateful odour of food gave hope to the hungry student. His guide opened the door of the cottage; he followed her in, and saw a woman bending over a fire in the middle of the floor. On the fire lay a large fish broiling. The daughter spoke a few words, and the mother turned and welcomed the stranger. She had an old and very wrinkled, but honest face, and looked troubled. She dusted the only chair in the cottage, and placed it for him by the side of the fire, opposite the one window, whence he saw a little patch of yellow sand over which the spent waves spread themselves out listlessly. Under this window there was a bench, upon which the daughter threw herself in an unusual posture, resting her chin upon her hand. A moment after, the youth caught the first glimpse of her blue eyes. They were fixed upon him with a strange look of greed, amounting to craving, but as if aware that they belied or betrayed her, she dropped them instantly. The moment she veiled them, her face, notwithstanding its colourless complexion, was almost beautiful.

When the fish was ready, the old woman wiped the deal table, steadied it upon the uneven floor, and covered it with a piece of fine table-linen. She then laid the fish on a wooden platter, and invited the guest to help himself. Seeing no other provision, he pulled from his pocket a hunting knife, and divided a portion from the fish, offering it to the mother first.

"Come, my lamb," said the old woman; and the daughter approached the table. But her nostrils and mouth quivered with disgust.

The next moment she turned and hurried from the hut.

"She doesn't like fish," said the old woman, "and I haven't anything else to give her."

"She does not seem in good health," he rejoined.

The woman answered only with a sigh, and they

ate their fish with the help of a little rye-bread. As they finished their supper, the youth heard the sound as of the pattering of a dog's feet upon the sand close to the door; but ere he had time to look out of the window, the door opened and the young woman entered. She looked better, perhaps from having just washed her face. She drew a stool to the corner of the fire opposite him. But as she sat down, to his bewilderment, and even horror, the student spied a single drop of blood on her white skin within her torn dress. The woman brought out a jar of whisky, put a rusty old kettle on the fire, and took her place in front of it. As soon as the water boiled, she proceeded to make some toddy in a wooden bowl.

Meantime the youth could not take his eyes off the young woman, so that at length he found himself fascinated, or rather bewitched. She kept her eyes for the most part veiled with the loveliest eyelids fringed with darkest lashes, and he gazed entranced; for the red glow of the little oil-lamp covered all the strangeness of her complexion. But as soon as he met a stolen glance out of those eyes unveiled, his soul shuddered within him. Lovely face and craving eyes alternated fascination and repulsion.

The mother placed the bowl in his hands. He drank sparingly, and passed it to the girl. She lifted it to her lips, and as she tasted—only tasted it—looked at him. He thought the drink must have been drugged and have affected his brain. Her hair smoothed itself back, and drew her forehead backwards with it; while the lower part of her face projected towards the bowl, revealing, ere she sipped, her dazzling teeth in strange prominence. But the same moment the vision vanished; she returned the vessel to her mother, and rising, hurried out of the cottage.

Then the old woman pointed to a bed of heather in one corner with a murmured apology; and the stu-

dent, wearied both with the fatigues of the day and
the strangeness of the night, threw himself upon it,
wrapped in his cloak. The moment he lay down, the
storm began afresh, and the wind blew so keenly
through the crannies of the hut, that it was only by
drawing his cloak over his head that he could protect
himself from its currents. Unable to sleep, he lay listening to the uproar, which grew in violence, till the
spray was dashing against the window. At length the
door opened, and the young woman came in, made
up the fire, drew the bench before it, and lay down
in the same strange posture, with her chin propped
on her hand and elbow, and her face turned towards
the youth. He moved a little; she dropped her head,
and lay on her face, with her arms crossed beneath
her forehead. The mother had disappeared.

Drowsiness crept over him. A movement of the
bench roused him, and he fancied he saw some four-
footed creature as tall as a large dog trot quietly out
of the door. He was sure he felt a rush of cold wind.
Gazing fixedly through the darkness, he thought he
saw the eyes of the damsel encountering his, but a
glow from the falling together of the remnants of the
fire, revealed clearly enough that the bench was vacant. Wondering what could have made her go out in
such a storm, he fell fast asleep.

In the middle of the night he felt a pain in his
shoulder, came broad awake, and saw the gleaming
eyes and grinning teeth of some animal close to his
face. Its claws were in his shoulder, and its mouth
in the act of seeking his throat. Before it had fixed its
fangs, however, he had its throat in one hand, and
sought his knife with the other. A terrible struggle
followed; but regardless of the tearing claws, he found
and opened his knife. He had made one futile stab,
and was drawing it for a surer, when, with a spring
of the whole body, and one wildly-contorted effort,

the creature twisted its neck from his hold, and with something betwixt a scream and a howl, darted from him. Again he heard the door open; again the wind blew in upon him, and it continued blowing; a sheet of spray dashed across the floor, and over his face. He sprung from his couch and bounded to the door.

It was a wild night—dark, but for the flash of whiteness from the waves as they broke within a few yards of the cottage; the wind was raving, and the rain pouring down the air. A gruesome sound as of mingled weeping and howling came from somewhere in the dark. He turned again into the hut and closed the door, but could find no way of securing it.

The lamp was nearly out, and he could not be certain whether the form of the young woman was upon the bench or not. Overcoming a strong repugnance, he approached it, and put out his hands—there was nothing there. He sat down and waited for the daylight: he dared not sleep any more.

When the day dawned at length, he went out yet again, and looked around. The morning was dim and gusty and gray. The wind had fallen, but the waves were tossing wildly. He wandered up and down the little strand, longing for more light.

At length he heard a movement in the cottage. By and by the voice of the old woman called to him from the door.

"You're up early, sir. I doubt you didn't sleep well."

"Not very well," he answered. "But where is your daughter?"

"She's not awake yet," said the mother. "I'm afraid I have but a poor breakfast for you. But you'll take a dram and a bit of fish. It's all I've got."

Unwilling to hurt her, though hardly in good appetite, he sat down at the table. While they were eating, the daughter came in, but turned her face away and went to the further end of the hut. When she came forward after a minute or two, the youth saw that her hair was drenched, and her face whiter than before. She looked ill and faint, and when she raised her eyes, all their fierceness had vanished, and sadness had taken its place. Her neck was now covered with a cotton handkerchief. She was modestly attentive to him, and no longer shunned his gaze. He was gradually yielding to the temptation of braving another night in the hut, and seeing what would follow, when the old woman spoke.

"The weather will be broken all day, sir," she said. "You had better be going, or your friends will leave without you."

Ere he could answer, he saw such a beseeching glance on the face of the girl, that he hesitated, con-

7

fused. Glancing at the mother, he saw the flash of wrath in her face. She rose and approached her daughter, with her hand lifted to strike her. The young woman stooped her head with a cry. He darted round the table to interpose between them. But the mother had caught hold of her; the handkerchief had fallen from her neck; and the youth saw five blue bruises on her lovely throat—the marks of the four fingers and the thumb of a left hand. With a cry of horror he darted from the house, but as he reached the door he turned. His hostess was lying motionless on the floor, and a huge gray wolf came bounding after him.

There was no weapon at hand; and if there had been, his inborn chivalry would never have allowed him to harm a woman even under the guise of a wolf. Instinctively, he set himself firm, leaning a little forward, with half-outstretched arms, and hands curved ready to clutch again at the throat upon which he had left those pitiful marks. But the creature as she sprung eluded his grasp, and just as he expected to feel her fangs, he found a woman weeping on his bosom, with her arms around his neck. The next instant, the gray wolf broke from him, and bounded howling up the cliff. Recovering himself as he best might, the youth followed, for it was the only way to the moor above, across which he must now make his way to find his companions.

All at once he heard the sound of a crunching of bones—not as if a creature was eating them, but as if they were ground by the teeth of rage and disappointment; looking up, he saw close above him the mouth of the little cavern in which he had taken refuge the day before. Summoning all his resolution, he passed it slowly and softly. From within came the sounds of a mingled moaning and growling.

Having reached the top, he ran at full speed for some distance across the moor before venturing to look behind him. When at length he did so, he saw,

He saw, against the sky,
the girl standing
on the edge of the cliff.

against the sky, the girl standing on the edge of the cliff, wringing her hands. One solitary wail crossed the space between. She made no attempt to follow him, and he reached the opposite shore in safety.

THE CRUEL PAINTER

AMONG the young men assembled at the University of Prague, in the year 159-, was one called Karl von Wolkenlicht. A somewhat careless student, he yet held a fair position in the estimation of both professors and men, because he could hardly look at a proposition without understanding it. Where such proposition, however, had to do with anything relating to the deeper insights of the nature, he was quite content that, for him, it should remain a proposition; which, however, he laid up in one of his mental cabinets, and was ready to reproduce at a moment's notice. This mental agility was more than matched by the corresponding corporeal excellence, and both aided in producing results in which his remarkable strength was equally apparent. In all games depending upon the combination of muscle and skill, he had scarce rivalry enough to keep him in practice. His strength, however, was embodied in such a softness of muscular outline, such a rare Greek-like style of beauty, and associated with such gentleness of manner and behaviour, that, partly from the truth of the resemblance, partly from the absurdity of the contrast, he was known throughout the university by the diminutive of the feminine form of his name, and was always called Lottchen.

"I say, Lottchen," said one of his fellow-students,

Reprinted from *Adela Cathcart* (1864).

called Richter, across the table in a wine-cellar they were in the habit of frequenting, "do you know, Heinrich Höllenrachen here says that he saw this morning, with mortal eyes, whom do you think?—Lilith."

"Adam's first wife?" asked Lottchen, with an attempt at carelessness, while his face flushed like a maiden's.

"None of your chaff!" said Richter. "Your face is honester than your tongue, and confesses what you cannot deny, that you would give your chance of salvation—a small one to be sure, but all you've got—for one peep at Lilith. Wouldn't you now, Lottchen?"

"Go to the devil!" was all Lottchen's answer to his tormentor; but he turned to Heinrich, to whom the students had given the surname above mentioned, because of the enormous width of his jaws, and said with eagerness and envy, disguising them as well as he could, under the appearance of curiosity:

"You don't mean it, Heinrich? You've been taking the beggar in! Confess now."

"Not I. I saw her with my two eyes."

"Notwithstanding the different planes of their orbits," suggested Richter.

"Yes, notwithstanding the fact that I can get a parallax to any of the fixed stars in a moment, with only the breadth of my nose for the base," answered Heinrich, responding at once to the fun, and careless of the personal defect insinuated. "She was near enough for even me to see her perfectly."

"When? Where? How?" asked Lottchen.

"Two hours ago. In the churchyard of St. Stephen's. By a lucky chance. Any more little questions, my child?" answered Höllenrachen.

"What could have taken her there, who is seen nowhere?" said Richter.

"She was seated on a grave. After she left, I went to the place; but it was a new-made grave. There was no stone up. I asked the sexton about her. He said he supposed she was the daughter of the woman buried there last Thursday week. I knew it was Lilith."

"Her mother dead?" said Lottchen, musingly. Then he thought with himself—"She will be going there again, then!" But he took care that this ghost-thought should wander unembodied. "But how did you know her, Heinrich? You never saw her before."

"How do you come to be over head and ears in love with her, Lottchen, and you haven't seen her at all?" interposed Richter.

"Will you or will you not go to the devil?" rejoined Lottchen, with a comic *crescendo*; to which the other replied with a laugh.

"No one could miss knowing her," said Heinrich.

"Is she so very like, then?"

"It is always herself, her very self."

A fresh flask of wine, turning out to be not up to the mark, brought the current of conversation against itself; not much to the dissatisfaction of Lottchen, who had already resolved to be in the churchyard of St. Stephen's at sun-down the following day, in the hope that he too might be favoured with a vision of Lilith.

This resolution he carried out. Seated in a porch of the church, not knowing in what direction to look for the apparition he hoped to see, and desirous as well of not seeming to be on the watch for one, he was gazing at the fallen rose-leaves of the sunset, withering away upon the sky; when, glancing aside by an involuntary movement, he saw a woman seated upon a new-made grave, not many yards from where he sat, with her face buried in her hands, and apparently weeping bitterly. Karl was in the shadow of the porch, and could see her perfectly, without much danger of being discovered by her; so he sat and watched her. She raised her head for a moment, and

13

the rose-flush of the west fell over it, shining on the tears with which it was wet, and giving the whole a bloom which did not belong to it, for it was always pale, and now pale as death. It was indeed the face of Lilith, the most celebrated beauty of Prague.

Again she buried her face in her hands; and Karl sat with a strange feeling of helplessness, which grew as he sat; and the longing to help her whom he could not help, drew his heart towards her with a trembling reverence which was quite new to him. She wept on. The western roses withered slowly away, and the clouds blended with the sky, and the stars gathered like drops of glory sinking through the vault of night, and the trees about the church yard grew black, and Lilith almost vanished in the wide darkness. At length she lifted her head, and seeing the night around her, gave a little broken cry of dismay. The minutes had swept over her head, not through her mind, and she did not know that the dark had come.

Hearing her cry, Karl rose and approached her. She heard his footsteps, and started to her feet. Karl spoke—

"Do not be frightened," he said. "Let me see you home. I will walk behind you."

"Who are you?" she rejoined.

"Karl Wolkenlicht."

"I have heard of you. Thank you. I can go home alone."

Yet, as if in a half-dreamy, half-unconscious mood, she accepted his offered hand to lead her through the graves, and allowed him to walk beside her, till, reaching the corner of a narrow street, she suddenly bade him good-night and vanished. He thought it better not to follow her, so he returned her good-night and went home.

How to see her again was his first thought the next day; as, in fact, how to see her at all had been

14

his first thought for many days. She went nowhere that ever he heard of; she knew nobody that he knew; she was never seen at church, or at market; never seen in the street. Her home had a dreary, desolate aspect. It looked as if no one ever went out or in. It was like a place on which decay had fallen because there was no indwelling spirit. The mud of years was baked upon its door, and no faces looked out of its dusty windows.

How then could she be the most celebrated beauty of Prague? How, then, was it that Heinrich Höllenrachen knew her the moment he saw her? Above all, how was it that Karl Wolkenlicht had, in fact, fallen in love with her before ever he saw her? It was thus:

Her father was a painter. Belonging thus to the public, it had taken the liberty of re-naming him. Every one called him Teufelsbürst, or Devilsbrush. It was a name with which, to judge from the nature of his representations, he could hardly fail to be pleased. For, not as a nightmare-dream, which may alternate with the loveliest visions, but as his ordinary everyday work, he delighted to represent human suffering.

Not an aspect of human woe or torture, as expressed in countenance or limb, came before his willing imagination, but he bore it straightway to his easel. In the moments that precede sleep, when the black space before the eyes of the poet teems with lovely faces, or dawns into a spirit-landscape, face after face of suffering, in all varieties of expression, would crowd, as if compelled by the accompanying fiends, to present themselves, in awful levée, before the inner eye of the expectant master. Then he would rise, light his lamp, and, with rapid hand, make notes of his visions; recording with swift successive sweeps of his pencil, every individual face which had rejoiced his evil fancy. Then he would return to his couch, and, well satisfied, fall asleep, to dream yet further embodiments of human ill.

What wrong could man or mankind have done him, to be thus fearfully pursued by the vengeance of the artist's hate?

Another characteristic of the faces and forms which he drew was, that they were all beautiful in the original idea. The lines of each face, however distorted by pain, would have been, in rest, absolutely beautiful; and the whole of the execution bore witness to the fact that upon this original beauty the painter had directed the artillery of anguish, to bring down the sky-soaring heights of its divinity to the level of a hated existence. To do this, he worked in perfect accordance with artistic law, falsifying no line of the original forms. It was the suffering, rather than his pencil, that wrought the change. The latter was the willing instrument to record what the imagination conceived with a cruelty composed enough to be correct.

To enhance the beauty he had thus distorted, and so to enhance yet further the suffering that produced the distortion, he would often represent attendant demons, whom he made as ugly as his imagination could compass; avoiding, however, all grotesqueness beyond what was sufficient to indicate that they were demons, and not men. Their ugliness rose from hate, envy, and all evil passions; amongst which he especially delighted to represent a gloating exultation over human distress. And often in the midst of his clouds of demon faces, would some one who knew him recognise the painter's own likeness, such as the mirror might have presented it to him when he was busiest over the incarnation of some exquisite torture.

But, apparently with the wish to avoid being supposed to choose such representations for their own sakes, he always found a story, often in the histories of the church, whose name he gave to the painting, and which he pretended to have inspired the pictorial conception. No one, however, who looked upon his suffering martyrs, could suppose for a moment that he honoured their martyrdom. They were but the vehicles for his hate of humanity. He was the torturer, and not Diocletian or Nero.

But, stranger yet to tell, there was no picture, whatever its subject, into which he did not introduce one form of placid and harmonious loveliness. In this, however, his fierceness was only more fully displayed. For in no case did this form manifest any relation either to the actors or the endurers in the picture. Hence its very loveliness became almost hateful to those who beheld it. Not a shade crossed the still sky of that brow, not a ripple disturbed the still sea of that cheek. She did not hate, she did not love the sufferers: the painter would not have her hate, for that would be to the injury of her loveliness; would not have her love, for he hated. Sometimes she floated above, as a still, unobservant angel, her gaze turned upward, dreaming along, careless as a white summer cloud, across the blue. If she looked down on the scene below, it was only that the beholder might see that she saw and did not care—that not a feather of her outspread pinions would quiver at the sight. Sometimes she would stand in the crowd, as if she had been copied there from another picture, and had nothing to do with this one, nor any right to be in it at all. Or when the red blood was trickling drop by drop from the crushed limb, she might be seen standing nearest, smiling over a primrose or the bloom on a peach. Some had said that she was the painter's wife; that she had been false to him; that he had killed her; and, finding that that was no sufficing revenge, thus half in love, and half in deepest hate, immortalized his vengeance. But it was now univer-

17

sally understood that it was his daughter, of whose loveliness extravagant reports went abroad; though all said, doubtless reading this from her father's pictures, that she was a beauty without a heart. Strange theories of something else supplying its place were rife among the anatomical students. With the girl in the pictures, the wild imagination of Lottchen, probably in part from her apparently absolute unattainableness and her undisputed heartlessness, had fallen in love, as far as the mere imagination can fall in love.

But again, how was he to see her? He haunted the house night after night. Those blue eyes never met his. No step responsive to his came from that door. It seemed to have been so long unopened that it had grown as fixed and hard as the stones that held its bolts in their passive clasp. He dared not watch in the day-time, and with all his watching at night, he never saw father or daughter or domestic cross the threshold. Little he thought that, from a shot-window near the door, a pair of blue eyes, like Lilith's, but paler and colder, were watching him, just as a spider watches the fly that is likely ere long to fall into his toils. And into those toils Karl soon fell. For her form darkened the page; her form stood on the threshold of sleep; and when, overcome with watching, he did enter its precincts, her form entered with him, and walked by his side. He must find her; or the world might go to the bottomless pit for him. But how?

Yes. He would be a painter. Teufelsbürst would receive him as a humble apprentice. He would grind his colours, and Teufelsbürst would teach him the mysteries of the science which is the handmaiden of art. Then he might see *her*, and that was all his ambition.

In the clear morning light of a day in autumn, when the leaves were beginning to fall seared from the hand of that Death which has his dance in the chapels of nature as well as in the cathedral aisles of men—he walked up and knocked at the dingy door. The spider painter opened it himself. He was a little man, meagre and pallid, with those faded blue eyes, a low nose in three distinct divisions, and thin, curveless, cruel lips. He wore no hair on his face; but long grey locks, long as a woman's, were scattered over his shoulders, and hung down on his breast. When Wolkenlicht had explained his errand, he smiled a smile in which hypocrisy could not hide the cunning, and, after many difficulties, consented to receive him as a pupil, on condition that he would become an inmate of his house. Wolkenlicht's heart bounded with delight, which he tried to hide: the second smile of Teufelsbürst might have shown him that he had ill succeeded. The fact that he was not a native of Prague, but, coming from a distant part of the country, was entirely his own master in the city, rendered this condition perfectly easy to fulfil; and that very afternoon, he entered the studio of Teufelsbürst as his scholar and servant.

It was a great room, filled with the appliances and results of art. Many pictures, festooned with cobwebs, were hung carelessly on the dirty walls. Others, half finished, leaned against them, on the floor. Several, in different stages of progress, stood upon easels. But all spoke the cruel bent of the artist's genius. In one corner a lay-figure was extended on a couch, covered with a pall of black velvet. Through its folds, the form beneath was easily discernible; and one hand and fore-arm protruded from beneath it, at right angles to the rest of the frame. Lottchen could not help shuddering when he saw it. Although he overcame the feeling in a moment, he felt a great repugnance to seating himself with his back towards it, as the arrangement of an easel, at which Teufelsbürst wished him to draw, rendered necessary. He contrived to edge himself round, so that when he lifted his eyes he should see the figure, and be sure that it could not rise without his being aware of it. But his master saw and understood his altered position; and under some pretence about the light, compelled him to resume the position in which he had placed him at first; after which he sat watching, over the top of his picture, the expression of his countenance as he tried to draw; reading in it the horrid fancy that the figure under the pall had risen, and was stealthily approaching to look over his shoulder. But Lottchen resisted the feeling, and, being already no contemptible draughtsman, was soon interested enough to forget it. And then, any moment, *she* might enter.

Now began a system of slow torture, for the chance of which the painter had been long on the watch— especially since he had first seen Karl lingering about the house. His opportunities of seeing physical suffering were nearly enough even for the diseased necessities of his art; but now he had one in his power, on whom, his own will fettering him, he could try any experiments he pleased for the production of a kind of suffering, in the observation of which he did not consider that he had yet had sufficient experience. He would hold the very heart of the youth in his hand, and wring it and torture it to his own content. And lest Karl should be strong enough to prevent those expressions of pain for which he lay on the watch, he would make use of further means, known to himself, and known to few besides.

All that day Karl saw nothing of Lilith; but he heard her voice once—and that was enough for one day. The next, she was sitting for her father the greater part of the day, and he could see her as often as he dared glance up from his drawing. She had looked at him when she entered, but had shown no sign of recognition; and all day long she took no further no-

tice of him. He hoped, at first, that this came of the
intelligence of love; but he soon began to doubt it.
For he saw that, with the holy shadow of sorrow, all
that distinguished the expression of her countenance
from that which the painter so constantly repro-
duced, had vanished likewise. It was the very face of
the unheeding angel whom, as often as he lifted his
eyes higher than hers, he saw on the wall above her,
playing on a psaltery in the smoke of the torment
ascending for ever from burning Babylon.—The power
of the painter had not merely wrought for the repre-
sentation of the woman of his imagination: it had had
scope as well in realizing her.

Karl soon began to see that communication, other
than of the eyes, was all but hopeless; and to any
attempt in that way she seemed altogether indisposed
to respond. Nor, if she had wished it, would it have
been safe; for as often as he glanced towards her,
instead of hers, he met the blue eyes of the painter,
gleaming upon him like winter-lightning. His tones,
his gestures, his words, seemed kind: his glance and
his smile refused to be disguised.

The first day he dined alone in the studio, waited
upon by an old woman; the next he was admitted to
the family table, with Teufelsbürst and Lilith. The
room offered a strange contrast to the study. As far
as handicraft, directed by a sumptuous taste, could
construct a house-paradise, this was one. But it
seemed rather a paradise of demons; for the walls
were covered with Teufelsbürst's paintings. During
the dinner Lilith's gaze scarcely met that of Wolkenlicht; and once or twice, when their eyes did meet,
her glance was so perfectly unconcerned, that Karl
wished he might look at her for ever without the fear
of her looking at him again. She seemed like one
whose love had rushed out glowing with seraphic
fire, to be frozen to death in a more than wintry cold:

GEORGE MACDONALD

she now walked lonely without her love. In the evenings, he was expected to continue his drawing by
lamplight; and at night he was conducted by Teufelsbürst to his chamber. Not once did he leave him there
without locking and bolting the door on the outside.
But he felt nothing except the coldness of Lilith.

Day after day she sat for her father, in every variety
of costume that could best show the variety of her
beauty. How much greater that beauty might be, if it
ever blossomed into a beauty of soul, Wolkenlicht
never imagined; for he soon loved her enough to at-
tribute to her all the possibilities of her face as actual
possessions of her being. To account for everything
that seemed to contradict this perfection, his brain
was prolific in inventions; till he was compelled at
last to see that she was in the condition of a rose-
bud, which, on the point of blossoming, has been
chilled into a changeless bud by the cold of an un-
timely frost. For one day, after the father and daughter
had become a little more accustomed to his silent
presence, a conversation began between them, which
went on until he saw that Teufelsbürst believed in
nothing except his art. How much of his feeling for
that could be dignified by the name of belief, seeing
its objects were such as they were, might have been
questioned. It seemed to Wolkenlicht to amount only
to this: that, amidst a thousand distastes, it was a
pleasant thing to re-produce on the canvas the forms
he beheld around him, modifying them to express the
prevailing feelings of his own mind.

A more desolate communication between souls
than that which then passed between father and
daughter could hardly be imagined. The father spoke
of humanity and all its experiences in a tone of the
bitterest scorn. He despised men and himself amongst
them; and rejoiced to think that the generations rose
and vanished, brood after brood, as the crops of corn

22

grew and disappeared. Lilith, who listened to it all unmoved, taking only an intellectual interest in the question, remarked that even the corn had more life than that; for, after its death, it rose again in the new crop. Whether she meant that the corn was therefore superior to man, forgetting that the superior can produce being without losing its own, or only advanced an objection to her father's argument, Wolkenlicht could not tell. But Teufelsbürst laughed like the sound of a saw, and said: "Follow out the analogy, my Lilith, and you will see that man is like the corn that springs again after it is buried; but unfortunately the only result we know of is a vampire."

Wolkenlicht looked up, and saw a shudder pass through the frame, and over the pale thin face of the painter. This he could not account for. But Teufelsbürst could have explained it, for there were strange whispers abroad, and they had reached his ear; and his philosophy was not quite enough for them. But the laugh with which Lilith met this frightful attempt at wit, grated dreadfully on Wolkenlicht's feeling. With her, too, however, a reaction seemed to follow. For, turning round a moment after, and looking at the picture on which her father was working, the tears rose in her eyes, and she said: "Oh! father, how like my mother you have made me this time!" "Child!" retorted the painter with a cold fierceness, "you have no mother. That which is gone out is gone out. Put no name in my hearing on that which is not. Where no substance is, how can there be a name?"

Lilth rose and left the room. Wolkenlicht now understood that Lilith was a frozen bud, and could not blossom into a rose. But pure love lives by faith. It loves the vaguely beheld and unrealized ideal. It dares believe that the loved is not all that she ever seemed. It is in virtue of this that love lives on. And it was in virtue of this, that Wolkenlicht loved Lilith yet more after he discovered what a grave of misery her unbelief was digging for her within her own soul. For her sake he would bear anything—bear even with calmness the torments of his own love; he would stay on, hoping and hoping.—The text, that we know not what a day may bring forth, is just as true of good things as of evil things; and out of Time's womb the facts must come.

But with the birth of this resolution to endure, his suffering abated; his face grew more calm; his love, no less earnest, was less imperious; and he did not look up so often from his work when Lilith was present. The master could see that his pupil was more at ease, and that he was making rapid progress in his art. This did not suit his designs, and he would betake himself to his further schemes.

For this purpose he proceeded first to simulate a friendship for Wolkenlicht, the manifestations of which he gradually increased, until, after a day or two, he asked him to drink wine with him in the evening. Karl readily agreed. The painter produced some of his best; but took care not to allow Lilith to taste it; for he had cunningly prepared and mingled with it a decoction of certain herbs and other ingredients, exercising specific actions upon the brain, and tending to the inordinate excitement of those portions of it which are principally under the rule of the imagination. By the reaction of the brain during the operation of these stimulants, the imagination is filled with suggestions and images. The nature of these determined by the prevailing mood of the time. They are such as the imagination would produce of itself; but increased in number and intensity. Teufelsbürst, without philosophizing about it, called his preparation simply a love-philtre, a concoction well known by name, but the composition of which was the secret of only a few. Wolkenlicht had, of course, not the least suspicion of the treatment to which he was subjected.

Teufelsbürst was, however, doomed to fresh disappointment. Not that his potion failed in the anticipated effect, for now Karl's real sufferings began; but that such was the strength of Karl's will, and his fear of doing anything that might give a pretext for banishing him from the presence of Lilith, that he was able to conceal his feelings far too successfully for the satisfaction of Teufelsbürst's art. Yet he had to fetter himself with all the restraints that self-exhortation could load him with, to refrain from falling at the feet of Lilith and kissing the hem of her garment. For that, as the lowliest part of all that surrounded her, itself kissing the earth, seemed to come nearest within the reach of his ambition, and therefore to draw him the most.

No doubt the painter had experience and penetration enough to perceive that he was suffering intensely; but he wanted to see the suffering embodied in outward signs, bringing it within the region over which his pencil held sway. He kept on, therefore, trying one thing after another, and rousing the poor youth to agony; till to his other sufferings were added, at length, those of failing health; a fact which notified itself evidently enough even for Teufelsbürst, though its signs were not of the sort he chiefly desired. But Karl endured all bravely.

Meantime, for various reasons, he scarcely ever left the house.

I must now interrupt the course of my story to introduce another element.

A few years before the period of my tale, a certain shoemaker of the city had died under circumstances more than suggestive of suicide. He was buried, however, with such precautions, that six weeks elapsed before the rumour of the facts broke out; upon which rumour, not before, the most fearful reports began to be circulated, supported by what seemed to the people of Prague incontestable evidence. —A *spectrum* of the deceased appeared to multitudes of persons, playing horrible pranks, and occasioning indescribable consternation throughout the whole town. This went on till at last, about eight months after his burial, the magistrates caused his body to be dug up; when it was found in just the condition of the bodies of those who in the eastern countries of Europe are called *vampires*. They buried the corpse under the gallows; but neither the digging up nor the re-burying were of avail to banish the spectre. Again the spade and pick-axe were set to work, and the dead man, being found considerably improved in *condition* since his last interment, was, with various horrible indignities, burnt to ashes, "after which the *spectrum* was never seen more."

And a second epidemic of the same nature had broken out a little before the period to which I have brought my story.

About midnight, after a calm frosty day, for it was now winter, a terrible storm of wind and snow came on. The tempest howled frightfully about the house of the painter, and Wolkenlicht found some solace in listening to the uproar, for his troubled thoughts would not allow him to sleep. It raged on all the next three days, till about noon on the fourth day, when it suddenly fell, and all was calm. The following night, Wolkenlicht, lying awake, heard unaccountable noises in the next house, as of things thrown about, of kicking and fighting horses, and of opening and shutting gates. Flinging wide his lattice and looking out, the noise of howling dogs came to him from every quarter of the town. The moon was bright and the air was still. In a little while he heard the sounds of a horse going at full gallop round the house, so that it shook as if it would fall; and flashes of light shone into his room. How much of this may have been owing to the effect of the drugs on poor Lottchen's brain, I leave my readers to determine. But when the family met at breakfast in the morning, Teufelsbürst, who had been already out of doors, reported that he had found the marks of strange feet in the snow, all about the house and through the garden at the back; stating, as his belief, that the tracks must be continued over the roofs, for there was no passage otherwise. There was a wicked gleam in his eye as he spoke; and Lilith believed that he was only trying an experiment on Karl's nerves. He persisted that he had never seen any footprints of the sort before. Karl informed him of his experiences during the night; upon which Teufelsbürst looked a little graver still, and proceeded to tell them that the storm, whose snow was still covering the ground, had arisen the very moment that their next-door neighbour died, and had ceased as suddenly the moment he was buried, though it had raved furiously all the time of the funeral, so that "it made men's bodies quake and their teeth chatter in their heads." Karl had heard that the man, whose name was John Kuntz, was dead and buried. He knew that he had been a very wealthy, and therefore most respectable, alderman of the town; that he had been very fond of horses; and that he had died in consequence of a kick received from one of his own, as he was looking at his hoof. But he had not heard that, just before he died, a black cat "opened the case-ment with her nails, ran to his bed, and violently scratched his face and the bolster, as if she endeav-oured by force to remove him out of the place where he lay. But the cat afterwards was suddenly gone, and she was no sooner gone, but he breathed his last."

So said Teufelsbürst, as the reporter of the town-

27

GEORGE MACDONALD

talk. Lilith looked very pale and terrified; and it was
perhaps owing to this that the painter brought no
more tales home with him. There were plenty to bring,
but he heard them all and said nothing. The fact was
that the philosopher himself could not resist the in-
fection of the fear that was literally raging in the city;
and perhaps the reports that he himself had sold himself to the devil, had sufficient response from his own
evil conscience to add to the influence of the epidemic upon him. The whole place was infested with
the presence of the dead Kuntz, till scarce a man or
woman would dare to be alone. He strangled old men;
insulted women; squeezed children to death; knocked
out the brains of dogs against the ground; pulled up
posts; turned milk into blood; nearly killed a worthy
clergyman by breathing upon him the intolerable airs
of the grave, cold and malignant and noisome; and,
in short, filled the city with a perfect madness of fear,
so that every report was believed without the smallest doubt or investigation.

Though Teufelsbürst brought home no more of the
town-talk, the old servant was a faithful purveyor,
and frequented the news-mart assiduously. Indeed
she had some nightmare experiences of her own that
she was proud to add to the stock of horrors which
the city enjoyed with such a hearty community of
goods. For those regions were not far removed from
the very birth-place and home of the vampire. The
belief in vampires is the quintessential concentration
and embodiment of all the passion of fear in Hungary
and the adjacent regions. Nor of all the other inventions of the human imagination, has there ever been
one so perfect in crawling terror as this. Lilith and
Karl were quite familiar with the popular ideas on the
subject. It did not require to be explained to them,
that a vampire was a body retaining a kind of animal
life after the soul had departed. If any relation con-

tinued between it and the vanished ghost, it was only sufficient to make it restless in its grave. Possessed of vitality enough to keep it uncorrupted and pliant, its only instinct was a blind hunger for the sole food which could keep its awful life persistent—living human blood. Hence it, or if not it, a sort of semi-material exhalation of essence of it, retaining its form and material relations, crept from its tomb, and went roaming about till it found some one asleep, towards whom it had an attraction, founded on old affection. It sucked the blood of this unhappy being, transferring so much of its life to itself as a vampire could assimilate. Death was the certain consequence. If suspicion conjectured aright, and they opened the proper grave, the body of the vampire would be found perfectly fresh and plump, sometimes indeed of rather florid complexion;—with grown hair, eyes half open, and the stains of recent blood about its greedy leechlike lips. Nothing remained but to consume the corpse to ashes, upon which the vampire would show itself no more. But what added infinitely to the horror was the certainty that whoever died from the mouth of the vampire, wrinkled grandsire, or delicate maiden, must in turn rise from the grave, and go forth a vampire, to suck the blood of the dearest left behind. This was the generation of the vampire brood. Lilith trembled at the very name of the creature. Karl was too much in love to be afraid of anything. Yet the evident fear of the unbelieving painter took a hold of his imagination; and, under the influence of the potions of which he still partook unwittingly—when he was not thinking about Lilith, he was thinking about the vampire.

Meantime, the condition of things in the painter's household continued much the same for Wolkenlicht—work all day; no communication between the young people; the dinner and the wine; silent reading when work was done, with stolen glances many over the top of the book, glances that were never returned; the cold good-night; the locking of the door; the wakeful night and the drowsy morning. But at length a change came, and sooner than any of the party had expected. For, whether it was that the impatience of Teufelsbürst had urged him to yet more dangerous experiments, or that the continuance of those he had been so long employing had overcome at length the vitality of Wolkenlicht—one afternoon, as he was sitting at his work, he suddenly dropped from his chair, and his master hurrying to him in some alarm, found him rigid and apparently lifeless. Lilith was not in the study when this took place. In justice to Teufelsbürst, it must be confessed that he employed all the skill he was master of, which for beneficent purposes was not very great, to restore the youth; but without avail. At last, hearing the footsteps of Lilith, he desisted in some consternation; and that she might escape being shocked by the sight of a dead body where she had been accustomed to see a living one, he removed the lay figure from the couch, and laid Karl in its place, covering him with the black velvet pall. He was just in time. She started at seeing no on in Karl's place, and said:

"Where is your pupil, father?"

"Gone home," he answered, with a kind of convulsive grin.

She glanced round the room, caught sight of the lay figure where it had not been before, looked at the couch, and saw the pall yet heaved up from beneath, opened her eyes till the entire white sweep around the iris suggested a new expression of consternation to Teufelsbürst, though from a quarter whence he did not desire or look for it; and then, without a word, sat down to a drawing she had been busy upon the day before. But her father, glancing at her now, as

"Gone home,"
Teulfelsbürst answered,
with a kind of compulsive grin.

Wolkenlicht had used to do, could not help seeing
that she was frightfully pale. She showed no other
sign of uneasiness. As soon as he released her, she
withdrew, with one more glance, as she passed, at
the couch and the figure blocked out in black upon
it. She hastened to her chamber, shut and locked the
door, sat down on the side of the couch, and fell, not
a-weeping, but a-thinking. Was he dead? What did it
matter? They would all be dead soon. Her mother
was dead already. It was only that earth could not
bear more children, except she devoured those to
whom she had already given birth. But what if they
had to come back in another form, and live another
sad, hopeless, loveless life over again?—And so she
went on questioning, and receiving no replies; while
through all her thoughts passed and repassed the
eyes of Wolkenlicht, which she had often felt to be
upon her when she did not see them, wild with re-
pressed longing, the light of their love shining through
the veil of diffused tears, ever gathering and never
overflowing. Then came the pale face, so worship-
ping, so distant in its self-withdrawn devotion, slowly
dawning out of the vapours of her reverie. When it
vanished, she tried to see it again. It would not come
when she called it; but when her thoughts left knocking at the door of the lost and wandered away, out
came the pale, troubled, silent face again, gathering
itself up from some unknown nook in her world of
phantasy, and once more, when she tried to steady
it by the fixedness of her own regard, fading back into
the mist. So the phantasm of the dead drew near and
wooed, as the living had never dared.—What if there
were any good in loving? What if men and women did
not die all out, but some dim shade of each, like that
pale, mind-ghost of Wolkenlicht, floated through the
eternal vapours of chaos? And what if they might
sometimes cross each other's path, meet, know that

they met, love on? Would not that revive the withered
memory, fix the fleeting ghost, give a new habitation,
a body even, to the poor, unhoused wanderers, frozen
by the eternal frosts, no longer thinking beings, but
thoughts wandering through the brain of the "Mel-
ancholy Mass"? Back with the thought came the face
of the dead Karl, and the maiden threw herself on her
bed in a flood of bitter tears. She could have loved
him if he had only lived: she did love him, for he was
dead. But even in the midst of the remorse that followed,—for had she not killed him?—life seemed a
less hard and hopeless thing than before. For it is
love itself and not its responses or results that is the
soul of life and its pleasures.

Two hours passed ere she could again show herself
to her father, from whom she seemed in some new
way divided by the new feeling in which he did not,
and could not share. But at last, lest he should seek
her, and finding her, should suspect her thoughts,
she descended and sought him.—For there is a maid-
enliness in sorrow, that wraps her garments close
around her.—But he was not to be seen; the door of
the study was locked. A shudder passed through her
as she thought of what her father, who lost no opportunity of furthering his all but perfect acquaintance with the human form and structure, might be
about with the figure which she knew lay dead beneath that velvet pall, but which had arisen to haunt
the hollow caves and cells of her living brain. She
rushed away, and up once more to her silent room,
through the darkness which had now settled down
in the house; threw herself again on her bed, and lay
almost paralysed with horror and distress.

But Teufelsbürst was not about anything so frightful as she supposed, though something frightful
enough. I have already implied that Wolkenlicht was,
in form, as fine an embodiment of youthful manhood

33

as any old Greek republic could have provided one of its sculptors with as model for an Apollo. It is true, that to the eye of a Greek artist he would not have been more acceptable in consequence of the regimen he had been going through for the last few weeks; but the emaciation of Wolkenlicht's frame, and the consequent prominence of the muscles, indicating the pain he had gone through, were peculiarly attractive to Teufelsbürst.—He was busy preparing to take a cast of the body of his dead pupil, that it might aid to the perfection of his future labours.

He was deep in the artistic enjoyment of a form, at the same time so beautiful and strong, yet with the lines of suffering in every limb and feature, when his daughter's hand was laid on the latch. He started, flung the velvet drapery over the body, and went to the door. But Lilith had vanished. He returned to his labours. The operation took a long time, for he performed it very carefully. Towards midnight, he had finished encasing the body in a close-clinging shell of plaster, which, when broken off, and fitted together, would be the matrix to the form of the dead Wolkenlicht. Before leaving it to harden till the morning, he was just proceeding to strengthen it with an additional layer all over, when a flash of lightning, reflected in all its dazzle from the snow without, almost blinded him. A peal of long-drawn thunder followed; the wind rose; and just such a storm came on as had risen some time before at the death of Kuntz, whose spectre was still tormenting the city. The gnomes of terror, deep hidden in the caverns of Teufelsbürst's nature, broke out jubilant. With trembling hands he tried to cast the pall over the awful white chrysalis,—failed, and fled to his chamber. And there lay the studio naked to the eyes of the lightning, with its tortured forms throbbing out of the dark, and quivering, as with life, in the almost continuous palpitations of the light; while on the couch lay the motionless mass of whiteness, gleaming blue in the lightning, almost more terrible in its crude indications of the human form, than that which it enclosed. It lay there as if dropped from some tree of chaos, haggard with the snows of eternity—a huge misshapen nut, with a corpse for its kernel.

But the lightning would soon have revealed a more terrible sight still, had there been any eyes to behold it. At midnight, while a peal of thunder was just dying away in the distance, the crust of death flew asunder, rending in all directions; and, pale as his investiture, staring with ghastly eyes, the form of Karl started up, sitting on the couch. Had he not been far beyond ordinary men in strength, he could not thus have rent his sepulchre. Indeed, had Teufelsbürst been able to finish his task by the additional layer of gypsum which he contemplated, he must have died the moment life revived; although, so long as the trance lasted, neither the exclusion from the air, nor the practical solidification of the walls of his chest, could do him any injury. He had lain unconscious throughout the operations of Teufelsbürst, but now the catalepsy had passed away, possibly under the influence of the electric condition of the atmosphere. Very likely the strength he now put forth was intensified by a convulsive reaction of all the powers of life, as is not unfrequently the case in sudden awakenings from similar interruptions of vital activity. The coming to himself and the bursting of his case were simultaneous. He sat staring about him, with, of all his mental faculties, only his imagination awake, from which the thoughts that occupied it when he fell senseless had not yet faded. These thoughts had been compounded of feelings about Lilith, and speculations about the vampire that haunted the neighbourhood; and the fumes of the last drug of which he had partaken, still hovering in his brain, combined with these thoughts and fancies to generate the delusion that he had just broken from the embrace of his coffin, and risen, the last-born of the vampire-race. The sense of unavoidable obligation to fulfil his doom, was yet mingled with a faint flutter of joy, for he knew that he must go to Lilith. With a deep sigh, he rose, gathered up the pall of black velvet, flung it around him, stepped from the couch, and left the study to find her.

Meantime, Teufelsbürst had sufficiently recovered to remember that he had left the door of the studio unfastened, and that anyone entering would discover in what he had been engaged, which, in the case of his getting into any difficulty about the death of Karl, would tell powerfully against him. He was at the farther end of a long passage, leading from the house to the studio, on his way to make all secure, when Karl appeared at the door, and advanced towards him. The painter, seized with invincible terror, turned and fled. He reached his room, and fell senseless on the floor. The phantom held on its way, heedless.

Lilith, on gaining her room the second time, had thrown herself on her bed as before, and had wept herself into a troubled slumber. She lay dreaming— and dreadful dreams. Suddenly she awoke in one of those peals of thunder which tormented the high regions of the air, as a storm billows the surface of the ocean. She lay awake and listened. As it died away, she thought she heard, mingling with its last muffled murmurs, the sound of moaning. She turned her face towards the room in keen terror. But she saw nothing. Another light, long-drawn sigh reached her ear, and at the same moment a flash of lightning illumined the room. In the corner farthest from her bed, she spied a white face, nothing more. She was dumb and motionless with fear. Utter darkness followed, a dark-

ness that seemed to enter into her very brain. Yet she
felt that the face was slowly crossing the black gulf
of the room, and drawing near to where she lay. The
next flash revealed, as it bended over her, the ghastly
face of Karl, down which flowed fresh tears. The rest
of his form was lost in blackness. Lilith did not faint,
but it was the very force of her fear that seemed to
keep her alive. It became for the moment the atmosphere of her life. She lay trembling and staring at the
spot in the darkness where she supposed the face of
Karl still to be. But the next flash showed her the
face far off, looking at her through the panes of her
lattice-window.

For Lottchen, as soon as he saw Lilith, seemed to
himself to go through a second stage of awaking. Her
face made him doubt whether he could be a vampire
after all; for instead of wanting to bite her arm and
suck the blood, he all but fell down at her feet in a
passion of speechless love. The next moment he became aware that his presence must be at least very
undesirable to her; and in an instant he had reached
her window, which he knew looked upon a lower roof
that extended between two different parts of the
house, and before the next flash came, he had stepped
through the lattice and closed it behind him.

Believing his own room to be attainable from this
quarter, he proceeded along the roof in the direction
he judged best. The cold winter air by degrees restored him entirely to his right mind, and he soon
comprehended the whole of the circumstances in
which he found himself. Peeping through a window
he was passing, to see whether it belonged to his
room, he spied Teufelsbürst, who, at the very moment, was lifting his head from the faint into which
he had fallen at the first sight of Lottchen. The moon
was shining clear, and in its light the painter saw, to
his horror, the pale face staring in at his window. He

thought it had been there ever since he had fainted, and dropped again in a deeper swoon than before. Karl saw him fall, and the truth flashed upon him that the wicked artist took him for what he had believed himself to be when first he recovered from his trance—namely, the vampire of the former Karl Wolkenlicht. The moment he comprehended it, he resolved to keep up the delusion if possible. Meantime he was innocently preparing a new ingredient for the popular dish of horrors to be served at the ordinary of the city the next day. For the old servant's were not the only eyes that had seen him besides those of Teufelsbürst. What could be more like a vampire, dragging his pall after him, than this apparition of poor, half-frozen Lottchen, crawling across the roof? Karl remembered afterwards that he had heard the dogs howling awfully in every direction, as he crept along; but this was hardly necessary to make those who saw him conclude that it was the same phantasm of John Kuntz, which had been infesting the whole city, and especially the house next door to the painter's, which had been the dwelling of the respectable alderman who had degenerated into this most disreputable of moneyless vagabonds. What added to the consternation of all who heard of it, was the sickening conviction that the extreme measures which they had resorted to in order to free the city from the ghoul, beyond which nothing could be done, had been utterly unavailing, successful as they had proved in every other known case of the kind. For, urged as well by various horrid signs about his grave, which not even its close proximity to the altar could render a place of repose, they had opened it, had found in the body every peculiarity belonging to a vampire, had pulled it out with the greatest difficulty on account of a quite supernatural ponderosity; which rendered the horse which had killed him—a strong animal—

all but unable to drag it along, and had at last, after cutting it in pieces, and expending on the fire two hundred and sixteen great billets, succeeded in conquering its incombustibleness, and reducing it to ashes. Such, at least, was the story which had reached the painter's household, and was believed by many; and if all this did not compel the perturbed corpse to rest, what more could be done?

When Karl had reached his room, and was dressing himself, the thought struck him that something might be made of the report of the extreme weight of the body of old Kuntz, to favour the continuance of the delusion of Teufelsbürst, although he hardly knew yet to what use he could turn this delusion. He was convinced that he would have made no progress however long he might have remained in his house; and that he would have more chance of favour with Lilith if he were to meet her in any other circumstances whatever, than those in which he invariably saw her—namely, surrounded by her father's influences, and watched by her father's cold blue eyes.

As soon as he was dressed, he crept down to the studio, which was now quiet enough, the storm being over, and the moon filling it with her steady shine. In the corner lay in all directions the fragments of the mould which his own body had formed and filled. The bag of plaster and the bucket of water which the painter had been using stood beside. Lottchen gathered all the pieces together, and then making his way to an out-house where he had seen various odds and ends of rubbish lying, chose from the heap as many pieces of old iron and other metal as he could find. To these he added a few large stones from the garden. When he had got all into the studio, he locked the door, and proceeded to fit together the parts of the mould, filling up the hollow as he went on with the heaviest things he could get into it, and solidifying the whole by pouring in plaster; till, having at length completed it, and obliterated, as much as possible, the marks of joining, he left it to harden, with the conviction that now it would make a considerable impression on Teufelsbürst's imagination, as well as on his muscular sense. He then left everything else as nearly undisturbed as he could; and, knowing all the ways of the house, was soon in the street, without leaving any signs of his exit.

Karl soon found himself before the house in which his friend Höllenrachen resided. Knowing his studious habits, he had hoped to see his light still burning, nor was he disappointed. He contrived to bring him to his window, and a moment after, the door was cautiously opened.

"Why, Lottchen, where do you come from?"

"From the grave, Heinrich, or next door to it."

"Come in, and tell me all about it. We thought the old painter had made a model of you, and tortured you to death."

"Perhaps you were not far wrong. But get me a horn of ale, for even a vampire is thirsty, you know."

"A vampire!" exclaimed Heinrich, retreating a pace, and involuntarily putting himself upon his guard.

Karl laughed.

"My hand was warm, was it not, old fellow?" he said. "Vampires are cold, all but the blood."

"What a fool I am!" rejoined Heinrich. "But you know we have been hearing such horrors lately that a fellow may be excused for shuddering a little when a pale-faced apparition tells him at two o'clock in the morning that he is a vampire, and thirsty, too."

Karl told him the whole story; and the mental process of regarding it for the sake of telling it, revealed to him pretty clearly some of the treatment of which he had been unconscious at the time. Heinrich was quite sure that his suspicions were correct. And now the question was, what was to be done next.

"At all events," said Heinrich, "we must keep you out of the way for some time. I will represent to my landlady that you are in hiding from enemies, and her heart will rule her tongue. She can let you have a garret-room, I know; and I will do as well as I can to bear you company. We shall have time then to invent some plan of operation."

To this proposal Karl agreed with hearty thanks, and soon all was arranged. The only conclusion they could yet arrive at was, that somehow or other the old demon-painter must be tamed.

Meantime, how fared it with Lilith? She too had no doubt that she had seen the body-ghost of poor Karl, and that the vampire had, according to rule, paid her the first visit because he loved her best. This was horrible enough if the vampire were not really the person he represented; but if in any sense it were Karl himself, at least it gave some expectation of a more prolonged existence than her father had taught her to look for; and if love anything like her mother's still lasted, even along with the habits of a vampire, there was something to hope for in the future. And then, though he had visited her, he had not, as far as she was aware, deprived her of a drop of blood. She could not be certain that he had not bitten her, for she had been in such a strange condition of mind that she might not have felt it, but she believed that he had restrained the impulses of his vampire nature, and had left her, lest he should yet yield to them. She fell fast asleep; and, when morning came, there was not, as far as she could judge, one of those triangular leech-like perforations to be found upon her whole body. Will it be believed that the moment she was satisfied of this, she was seized by a terrible jealousy, lest Karl should have gone and bitten someone else?

Most people will wonder that she should not have gone out of her senses at once; but there was all the difference between a visit from a real vampire and a visit from a man she had begun to love, even although she took him for a vampire. All the difference does *not* lie in a name. They were very different causes, and the effects must be different.

When Teufelsbürst came down in the morning, he crept into the studio like a murderer. There lay the awful white block, seeming to his eyes just the same as he had left it. What was to be done with it? He dared not open it. Mould and model must go together. But whither? If inquiry should be made after Wolkenlicht, and this were discovered anywhere on his premises, would it not be enough to bring him at once to the gallows? Therefore it would be dangerous to bury it in the garden; or in the cellar.

"Besides," thought he, with a shudder, "that would be to fix the vampire as a guest for ever."—And the horrors of the past night rushed back upon his imagination with renewed intensity. What would it be to have the dead Karl crawling about his house for ever, now inside, now out, now sitting on the stairs, now staring in at the windows?

He would have dragged it to the bottom of his garden, past which the Moldau flowed, and plunged it into the stream; but then, should the spectre continue to prove troublesome, it would be almost impossible to reach the body so as to destroy it by fire; besides which, he could not do it without assistance, and the probability of discovery. If, however, the apparition should turn out to be no vampire, but only a respectable ghost, they might manage to endure its presence, till it should be weary of haunting them.

He resolved at last to convey the body for the meantime into a concealed cellar in the house, seeing something must be done before his daughter came down. Proceeding to remove it, his consternation was greatly increased when he discovered how the body had grown in weight since he had thus disposed of it, leaving on his mind scarcely a hope that it could turn out not to be a vampire after all. He could scarcely stir it, and there was but one whom he could call to his assistance—the old woman who acted as his housekeeper and servant.

He went to her room, roused her, and told her the whole story. Devoted to her master for many years, and not quite so sensitive to fearful influences as when less experienced in horrors, she showed immediate readiness to render him assistance. Utterly unable, however, to lift the mass between them, they could only drag and push it along; and such a slow toil was it that there was no time to remove the traces of its track, before Lilith came down and saw a broad white line leading from the door of the studio down the cellar-stairs. She knew in a moment what it meant; but not a word was uttered about the matter, and the name of Karl Wolkenlicht seemed to be entirely forgotten.

But how could the affairs of a house go on all the same when every one of the household knew that a dead body lay in the cellar?—nay more, that, although it lay still and dead enough all day, it would come half alive at nightfall, and, turning the whole house into a sepulchre by its presence, go creeping about like a cat all over it in the dark—perhaps with phosphorescent eyes? So it was not surprising that the painter abandoned his studio early, and that the three found themselves together in the gorgeous room formerly described, as soon as twilight began to fall.

Already Teufelsbürst had begun to experience a kind of shrinking from the horrid faces in his own pictures, and to feel disgusted at the abortions of his own mind. But all that he and the old woman now

43

felt was an increasing fear as the night drew on, a kind of sickening and paralysing terror. The thing down there would not lie quiet—at least its phantom in the cellars of their imagination would not. As much as possible, however, they avoided alarming Lilith, who, knowing all they knew, was as silent as they. But her mind was in a strange state of excitement, partly from the presence of a new sense of love, the pleasure of which all the atmosphere of grief into which it grew could not totally quench. It comforted her somehow, as a child may comfort when his father is away.

Bedtime came, and no one made a move to go. Without a word spoken on the subject, the three remained together all night; the elders nodding and slumbering occasionally, and Lilith getting some share of repose on a couch. All night the shape of death might be somewhere about the house; but it did not disturb them. They heard no sound, saw no sight; and when the morning dawned, they separated, chilled and stupid, and for the time beyond fear, to seek repose in their private chambers. There they remained equally undisturbed.

But when the painter approached his easel a few hours after, looking more pale and haggard still than he was wont, from the fears of the night, a new bewilderment took possession of him. He had been busy with a fresh embodiment of his favourite subject, into which he had sketched the form of the student as the sufferer. He had represented poor Wolkenlicht as just beginning to recover from a trance, while a group of surgeons, unaware of the signs of returning life, were absorbed in a minute dissection of one of the limbs. At an open door he had painted Lilith passing, with her face buried in a bunch of sweet-peas. But when he came to the picture, he found, to his astonishment and terror, that the face of one

of the group was now turned towards that of the vic-
tim, regarding his revival with demoniac satisfaction,
and taking pains to prevent the others from discov-
ering it. The face of this prince of torturers was that
of Teufelsbürst himself. Lilith had altogether vanished, and in her place stood the dim vampire reiter-
ation of the body that lay extended on the table, staring
greedily at the assembled company. With trembling
hands the painter removed the picture from the easel,
and turned its face to the wall.

Of course this was the work of Lottchen. When he
left the house, he took with him the key of a small
private door, which was so seldom used that, while
it remained closed, the key would not be missed, perhaps for many months. Watching the windows, he
had chosen a safe time to enter, and had been hard
at work all night on these alterations. Teufelsbürst
attributed them to the vampire, and left the picture
as he found it, not daring to put brush to it again.

The next night was passed much after the same
fashion. But the fear had begun to die away a little in
the hearts of the women, who did not know what had
taken place in the study on the previous night. It
burrowed, however, with gathered force in the vitals
of Teufelsbürst. But this night likewise passed in
peace; and before it was over, the old woman had
taken to speculating in her own mind as to the best
way of disposing of the body, seeing it was not at all
likely to be troublesome. But when the painter entered his study in trepidation the next morning, he
found that the form of the lovely Lilith was painted
out of every picture in the room. This could not be
concealed; and Lilith and the servant became aware
that the studio was the portion of the house in haunting which the vampire left the rest in peace.

Karl recounted all the tricks he had played to his
friend Heinrich, who begged to be allowed to bear

him company the following night. To this Karl consented, thinking it would be considerably more agreeable to have a companion. So they took a couple of
bottles of wine and some provisions with them, and
before midnight found themselves snug in the study.
They sat very quiet for some time, for they knew that
if they were seen, two vampires would not be so terrible as one, and might occasion discovery. But at
length Heinrich could bear it no longer.

"I say, Lottchen, let's go and look for your dead
body. What has the old beggar done with it?"

"I think I know. Stop; let me peep out. All right!
Come along."

With a lamp in his hand, he led the way to the
cellars, and after searching about a little, they discovered it.

"It looks horrid enough," said Heinrich, "but I think
a drop or two of wine would brighten it up a little."

So he took a bottle from his pocket, and after they
had had a glass apiece, he dropped a third in blots all
over the plaster. Being red wine, it had the effect Höllenrachen desired.

"When they visit it next, they will know that the
vampire can find the food he prefers," said he.

In a corner close by the plaster, they found the
clothes Karl had worn.

"Hillo!" said Heinrich, "we'll make something of
this find."

So he carried them with him to the study. There
he got hold of the lay-figure.

"What are you about, Heinrich?"

"Going to make a scarecrow to keep the ravens off
old Teufel's pictures," answered Heinrich, as he went
on dressing the lay-figure in Karl's clothes. He next
seated the creature at an easel with its back to the
door, so that it should be the first thing the painter
should see when he entered. Karl meant to remove

this before he went, for it was too comical to fall in with the rest of his proceedings. But the two sat down to their supper, and by the time they had finished the wine, they thought they should like to go to bed. So they got up and went home, and Karl forgot the lay-figure, leaving it in busy motionlessness all night before the easel.

When Teufelsbürst saw it, he turned and fled with a cry that brought his daughter to his help. He rushed past her, able only to articulate:

"The vampire! The vampire! Painting!"

Far more courageous than he, because her conscience was more peaceful, Lilith passed on to the studio. She too recoiled a step or two when she saw the figure; but with the sight of the back of Karl, as she supposed it to be, came the longing to see the face that was on the other side. So she crept round and round by the wall, as far off as she could. The figure remained motionless. It was a strange kind of shock that she experienced when she saw the face, disgusting from its inanity. The absurdity next struck her; and with the absurdity flashed into her mind the conviction that this was not the doing of a vampire; for of all creatures under the moon, he could not be expected to be a humourist. A wild hope sprang up in her mind that Karl was not dead. Of this she soon resolved to make herself sure.

She closed the door of the studio; in the strength of her new hope, undressed the figure, put it in its place, concealed the garments—all the work of a few minutes; and then, finding her father just recovering from the worst of his fear, told him there was nothing in the studio but what ought to be there, and persuaded him to go and see. He not only saw no one, but found that no further liberties had been taken with his pictures. Reassured, he soon persuaded himself that the spectre in this case had been the offspring of his own terror-haunted brain. But he had no spirit for painting now. He wandered about the house, himself haunting it like a restless ghost.

When night came, Lilith retired to her own room. The waters of fear had begun to subside in the house; but the painter and his old attendant did not yet follow her example.

As soon, however, as the house was quite still, Lilith glided noiselessly down the stairs, went into the studio, where as yet there assuredly was no vampire, and concealed herself in a corner.

As it would not do for an earnest student like Heinrich to be away from his work very often, he had not asked to accompany Lottchen this time. And indeed Karl himself, a little anxious about the result of the scarecrow, greatly preferred going alone.

While she was waiting for what might happen, the conviction grew upon Lilith, as she reviewed all the past of the story, that these phenomena were the work of the real Karl, and of no vampire. In a few moments she was still more sure of this. Behind the screen where she had taken refuge, hung one of the pictures out of which her portrait had been painted the night before last. She had taken a lamp with her into the study, with the intention of extinguishing it the moment she heard any sign of approach; but as the vampire lingered, she began to occupy herself with examining the picture beside her. She had not looked at it long, before she wetted the tip of her forefinger, and began to rub away at the obliteration. Her suspicions were instantly confirmed: the substance employed was only a gummy wash over the paint. The delight she experienced at the discovery threw her into a mischievous humour.

"I will see," she said to herself, "whether I cannot match Karl Wolkenlicht at this game."

In a closet in the room hung a number of costumes, which Lilith had at different times worn for her father. Among them was a large white drapery, which she easily disposed as a shroud. With the help of some chalk, she soon made herself ghastly enough, and then placing her lamp on the floor behind the screen, and setting a chair over it, so that it should throw no light in any direction, she waited once more for the vampire. Nor had she much longer to wait. She soon heard a door move, the sound of which she hardly knew, and then the studio door opened. Her heart beat dreadfully, not with fear lest it should be a vampire after all, but with hope that it was Karl. To see him once more was too great joy. Would she not make up to him for all her coldness! But would he care for her now? Perhaps he had been quite cured of his longing for a hard heart like hers. She peeped. It was he sure enough, looking as handsome as ever. He was holding his light to look at her last work, and the expression of his face, even in regarding her hand-iwork, was enough to let her know that he loved her still. If she had not seen this, she dared not have shown herself from her hiding-place. Taking the lamp in her hand, she got upon the chair, and looked over the screen, letting the light shine from below upon her face. She then made a slight noise to attract Karl's attention. He looked up, evidently rather startled, and saw the face of Lilith in the air. He gave a stifled cry, threw himself on his knees, with his arms stretched towards her, and moaned—

"I have killed her! I have killed her!"

Lilith descended, and approached him noiselessly. He did not move. She came close to him and said:

"Are you Karl Wolkenlicht?"

His lips moved, but no sound came.

"If you are a vampire, and I am a ghost," she said— but a low happy laugh alone concluded the sentence.

Karl sprang to his feet. Lilith's laugh changed into

a burst of sobbing and weeping, and in another moment the ghost was in the arms of the vampire.

Lilith had no idea how far her father had wronged Karl, and though, from thinking over the past, he had no doubt that the painter had drugged him, he did not wish to pain her by imparting this conviction. But Lilith was afraid of a reaction of rage and hatred in her father after the terror was removed; and Karl saw that he might thus be deprived of all further intercourse with Lilith, and all chance of softening the old man's heart towards him; while Lilith would not hear of forsaking him who had banished all the human race but herself. They managed at length to agree upon a plan of operation.

The first thing they did was to go to the cellar where the plaster mass lay, Karl carrying with him a great axe used for cleaving wood. Lilith shuddered when she saw it, stained as it was with the wine Heinrich had spilt over it, and almost believed herself the midnight companion of a vampire after all, visiting with him the terrible corpse in which he lived all day. But Karl soon reassured her; and a few good blows of the axe revealed a very different core to that which Teufelsbürst supposed to be in it. Karl broke it into pieces, and with Lilith's help, who insisted on carrying her share, the whole was soon at the bottom of the Moldau, and every trace of its ever having existed removed. Before morning, too, the form of Lilith had dawned anew in every picture. There was no time to restore to its former condition the one Karl had first altered; for in it the changes were all that they seemed; nor indeed was he capable of restoring it in the master's style; but they put it quite out of the way, and hoped that sufficient time might elapse before the painter thought of it again.

When they had done, and Lilith, for all his entreaties, would remain with him no longer, Karl took his former clothes with him, and having spent the rest of the night in his old room, dressed in them in the morning. When Teufelsbürst entered his studio next day, there sat Karl, as if nothing had happened, finishing the drawing on which he had been at work when the fit of insensibility came upon him. The painter started, stared, rubbed his eyes, thought it was another spectral illusion, but was on the point of yielding to his terror, when Karl rose, and approached him with a smile. The healthy, sunshiny countenance of Karl, let him be ghost or goblin, could not fail to produce somewhat of a tranquillizing effect on Teufelsbürst. He took his offered hand mechanically, his countenance utterly vacant with idiotic bewilderment. Karl said:

"I was not well, and thought it better to pay a visit to a friend for a few days; but I shall soon make up for lost time, for I am all right now."

He sat down at once, taking no notice of his master's behaviour, and went on with his drawing. Teufelsbürst stood staring at him for some minutes without moving, then suddenly turned and left the room. Karl heard him hurrying down the cellar stairs. In a few moments he came up again. Karl stole a glance at him. There he stood in the same spot, no doubt more full of bewilderment than ever; but it was not possible that his face should express more. At last he went to his easel, and sat down with a long-drawn sigh as if of relief. But though he sat at his easel, he painted none that day; and as often as Karl ventured a glance, he saw him still staring at him. The discovery that his pictures were restored to their former condition aided, no doubt, in leading him to the same conclusion as the other facts, whatever that conclusion might be—probably that he had been the sport of some evil power, and had been for the greater part of a week utterly bewitched. Lilith had taken care to instruct the old woman, with whom she was all-powerful; and as neither of them showed the smallest traces of the astonishment which seemed to be slowly vitrifying his own brain, he was at last perfectly satisfied that things had been going on all right everywhere but in his inner man; and in this conclusion he certainly was not far wrong in more senses than one. But when all was restored again to the old routine, it became evident that the peculiar direction of his art in which he had hitherto indulged had ceased to interest him. The shock had acted chiefly upon that part of his mental being which had been so absorbed. He would sit for hours without doing anything, apparently plunged in meditation.—Several weeks elapsed without any change, and both Lilith and Karl were getting dreadfully anxious about him. Karl paid him every attention; and the old man, for he now looked much older than before, submitted to receive his services as well as those of Lilith. At length, one morning, he said in a slow thoughtful tone:

"Karl Wolkenlicht, I should like to paint you."

"Certainly, sir," answered Karl, jumping up, "where would you like me to sit?"

So the ice of silence and inactivity was broken, and the painter drew and painted; and the spring of his art flowed once more; and he made a beautiful portrait of Karl—a portrait without evil or suffering. And as soon as he had finished Karl, he began once more to paint Lilith; and when he had painted her, he composed a picture for the very purpose of introducing them together; and in this picture there was neither ugliness nor torture, but human feeling and human hope instead. Then Karl knew that he might speak to him of Lilith; and he spoke, and was heard with a smile. But he did not dare to tell him the truth of the vampire story till one day that Teufelsbürst was lying on the floor of a room in Karl's ancestral castle, half smothered in grand-children; when the only answer it drew from the old man was a kind of shuddering laugh, and the words—"Don't speak of it, Karl, my boy!"

THE BROKEN SWORDS

THE eyes of three, two sisters and a brother, gazed for the last time on a great pale-golden star, that followed the sun down the steep west. It went down to arise again; and the brother about to depart might return, but more than the usual doubt hung upon his future. For between the white dresses of the sisters, shone his scarlet coat and golden swordknot, which he had put on for the first time, more to gratify their pride than his own vanity. The brightening moon, as if prophetic of a future memory, had already begun to dim the scarlet and the gold, and to give them a pale, ghostly hue. In her thoughtful light the whole group seemed more like a meeting in the land of shadows, than a parting in the substantial earth.—But which should be called the land of realities?—the region where appearance, and space, and time drive between, and stop the flowing currents of the soul's speech? or that region where heart meets heart, and appearance has become the slave to utterance, and space and time are forgotten?

Through the quiet air came the far-off rush of water, and the near cry of the land-rail. Now and then a chilly wind blew unheeded through the startled and jostling leaves that shaded the ivy-seat. Else, there was calm everywhere, rendered yet deeper and more intense by the dusky sorrow that filled their hearts.

Reprinted from *Monthly Christian Spectator* (1854).

For, far away, hundreds of miles beyond the hearing of their ears, roared the great war-guns; next week their brother must sail with his regiment to join the army; and to-morrow he must leave his home.

The sisters looked on him tenderly, with vague fears about his fate. Yet little they divined it. That the face they loved might lie pale and bloody, in a heap of slain, was the worst image of it that arose before them; but this, had they seen the future, they would, in ignorance of the further future, have infinitely preferred to that which awaited him. And even while they looked on him, a dim feeling of the unsuitableness of his lot filled their minds. For, indeed, to all judgments it must have seemed unsuitable that the home-boy, the loved of his mother, the pet of his sisters, who was happy, womanlike (as Coleridge says), if he possessed the signs of love, having never yet sought for its proofs—that he should be sent amongst soldiers, to command and be commanded; to kill, or perhaps to be himself crushed out of the fair earth in the uproar that brings back for the moment the reign of Night and Chaos. No wonder that to his sisters it seemed strange and sad. Yet such was their own position in the battle of life, in which their father had died with doubtful conquest, that when their old military uncle sent the boy an ensign's commission, they did not dream of refusing the only path open, as they thought, to an honourable profession, even though it might lead to the trench-grave. They heard it as the voice of destiny, wept, and yielded.

If they had possessed a deeper insight into his character, they would have discovered yet further reason to doubt the fitness of the profession chosen for him; and if they had ever seen him at school, it is possible the doubt of fitness might have strengthened into a certainty of incongruity. His comparative inactivity amongst his schoolfellows, though occa-

sioned by no dulness of intellect, might have suggested the necessity of a quiet life, if inclination
and liking had been the arbiters in the choice. Nor
was this inactivity the result of defective animal spirits either, for sometimes his mirth and boyish frolic
were unbounded; but it seemed to proceed from an
over-activity of the inward life, absorbing, and in some
measure checking, the outward manifestation. He had
so much to do in his own hidden kingdom, that he
had not time to take his place in the polity and strife
of the commonwealth around him. Hence, while other
boys were acting, he was thinking. In this point of
difference, he felt keenly the superiority of many of
his companions; for another boy would have the ob-
stacle overcome, or the adversary subdued, while he
was meditating on the propriety, or on the means, of
effecting the desired end. He envied their prompti-
tude, while they never saw reason to envy his wisdom; for his conscience, tender and not strong,
frequently transformed slowness of determination into
irresolution: while a delicacy of the sympathetic
nerves tended to distract him from any predeter-
mined course, by the diversity of their vibrations,
responsive to influences from all quarters, and
destructive to unity of purpose.

Of such a one, the *a priori* judgment would be,
that he ought to be left to meditate and grow for some
time, before being called upon to produce the fruits
of action. But add to these mental conditions a vivid
imagination, and a high sense of honour, nourished
in childhood by the reading of the old knightly romances, and then put the youth in a position in which
action is imperative, and you have elements of strife
sufficient to reduce that fair kingdom of his to utter
anarchy and madness. Yet so little do we know ourselves, and so different are the symbols with which
the imagination works its algebra, from the realities

which those symbols represent, that as yet the youth felt no uneasiness, but contemplated his new calling with a glad enthusiasm and some vanity; for all his prospect lay in the glow of the scarlet and the gold. Nor did this excitement receive any check till the day before his departure, on which day I have introduced him to my readers, when, accidentally taking up a newspaper of a week old, his eye fell on these words—*"Already crying women are to be met in the streets."* With this cloud afar on his horizon, which, though no bigger than a man's hand, yet cast a perceptible shadow over his mind, he departed next morning. The coach carried him beyond the consecrated circle of home laws and impulses, out into the great tumult, above which rises ever and anon the cry of Cain, "Am I my brother's keeper?"

Every tragedy of higher order, constructed in Christian times, will correspond more or less to the grand drama of the Bible; wherein the first act opens with a brilliant sunset vision of Paradise, in which childish sense and need are served with all the profusion of the indulgent nurse. But the glory fades off into grey and black, and night settles down upon the heart which, rightly uncontent with the childish, and not having yet learned the childlike, seeks knowledge and manhood as a thing denied by the Maker, and yet to be gained by the creature; so sets forth alone to climb the heavens, and instead of climbing, falls into the abyss. Then follows the long dismal night of feverish efforts and delirious visions, or, it may be, helpless despair; till at length a deeper stratum of the soul is heaved to the surface; and amid the first dawn of morning, the youth says within him, "I have sinned against my *Maker*—I will arise and go to my *Father*." More or less, I say, will Christian tragedy correspond to this—a fall and a rising again; not a rising only, but a victory; not a victory merely, but a triumph.

Such, in its way and degree, is my story. I have shown, in one passing scene, the home paradise; now I have to show a scene of a far differing nature.

The young ensign was lying in his tent, weary, but wakeful. All day long the cannon had been bellowing against the walls of the city, which now lay with wide, gaping breach, ready for the morrow's storm, but covered yet with the friendly darkness. His regiment was ordered to be ready with the earliest dawn to march up to the breach. That day, for the first time, there had been blood on his sword—there the sword lay, a spot on the chased hilt still. He had cut down one of the enemy in a skirmish with a sally party of the besieged, and the look of the man as he fell, haunted him. He felt, for the time, that he dared not pray to the Father, for the blood of a brother had rushed forth at the stroke of his arm, and there was one fewer of living souls on the earth because he lived thereon. And to-morrow he must lead a troop of men up to that poor disabled town, and turn them loose upon it, not knowing what might follow in the triumph of enraged and victorious foes, who for weeks had been subjected, by the constancy of the place, to the greatest privations. It was true the general had issued his commands against all disorder and pillage; but if the soldiers once yielded to temptation, what might not be done before the officers could reclaim them! All the wretched tales he had read of the sack of cities rushed back on his memory. He shuddered as he lay. Then his conscience began to speak, and to ask what right he had to be there.—Was the war a just one?— He could not tell; for this was a bad time for settling nice questions. But there he was, right or wrong, fighting and shedding blood on God's earth, beneath God's heaven.

Over and over he turned the question in his mind; again and again the spouting blood of his foe, and the death-look in his eye, rose before him; and the youth who at school could never fight with a companion because he was not sure that he was in the right, was alone in the midst of undoubting men of war, amongst whom he was driven helplessly along, upon the waves of a terrible necessity. What wonder that in the midst of these perplexities his courage should fail him! What wonder that the consciousness of fainting should increase the faintness! or that the dread of fear and its consequences should hasten and invigorate its attacks! To crown all, when he dropped into a troubled slumber at length, he found himself hurried, as on a storm of fire, through the streets of the captured town, from all the windows of which looked forth familiar faces, old and young, but distorted from the memory of his boyhood by fear and wild despair. On one spot lay the body of his father, with his face to the earth; and he woke at the cry of horror and rage that burst from his own lips, as he saw the rough, bloody hand of a soldier twisted in the loose hair of his elder sister, and the younger fainting in the arms of a scoundrel belonging to his own regiment.

He slept no more. As the grey morning broke, the troops appointed for the attack assembled without sound of trumpet or drum, and were silently formed in fitting order. The young ensign was in his place, weary and wretched after his miserable night. Before him he saw a great, broad-shouldered lieutenant, whose brawny hand seemed almost too large for his sword-hilt, and in any one of whose limbs played more animal life than in the whole body of the pale youth. The firm-set lips of this officer, and the fire of his eye, showed a concentrated resolution, which, by the contrast, increased the misery of the ensign, and seemed, as if the stronger absorbed the weaker, to draw out from him the last fibres of self-possession: the sight of unattainable determination, while it in-

creased the feeling of the arduousness of that which
required such determination, threw him into the great
gulf which lay between him and it. In this disorder
of his nervous and mental condition, with a doubting
conscience and a shrinking heart, is it any wonder
that the terrors which lay before him at the gap in
those bristling walls, should draw near, and, making
sudden inroad upon his soul, overwhelm the government of a will worn out by the tortures of an unas-
sured spirit? What share fear contributed to unman
him, it was impossible for him, in the dark, confused
conflict of differing emotions, to determine; but
doubtless a natural shrinking from danger, there being
no excitement to deaden its influence, and no hope
of victory to encourage to the struggle, seeing victory
was dreadful to him as defeat, had its part in the sad
result. Many men who have courage, are dependent
on ignorance and a low state of the moral feeling for
that courage; and a further progress towards the development of the higher nature would, for a time at
least, entirely overthrow it. Nor could such loss of
courage be rightly designated by the name of
cowardice.

But, alas! the colonel happened to fix his eyes upon
him as he passed along the file; and this completed
his confusion. He betrayed such evident symptoms
of perturbation, that that officer ordered him under
arrest; and the result was, that, chiefly for the sake
of example to the army, he was, upon trial by court-
martial, expelled from the service, and had his sword
broken over his head. Alas for the delicate-minded
youth! Alas for the home-darling!

Long after, he found at the bottom of his chest the
pieces of the broken sword, and remembered that, at
the time, he had lifted them from the ground and
carried them away. But he could not recall under
what impulse he had done so. Perhaps the agony he

suffered, passing the bounds of mortal endurance, had opened for him a vista into the eternal, and had shown him, if not the injustice of the sentence passed upon him, yet his freedom from blame, or, endowing him with dim prophetic vision, had given him the assurance that some day the stain would be wiped from his soul, and leave him standing clear before the tribunal of his own honour. Some feeling like this, I say, may have caused him, with a passing gleam of indignant protest, to lift the fragments from the earth, and carry them away; even as the friends of a so-called traitor may bear away his mutilated body from the wheel. But if such was the case, the vision was soon overwhelmed and forgotten in the succeeding anguish. He could not see that, in mercy to his doubting spirit, the question which had agitated his mind almost to madness, and which no results of the impending conflict could have settled for him, was thus quietly set aside for the time; nor that, painful as was the dark, dreadful existence that he was now to pass in self-torment and moaning, it would go by, and leave his spirit clearer far, than if, in his apprehension, it had been stained with further blood-guiltiness, instead of the loss of honour. Years after, when he accidentally learned that on that very morning the whole of his company, with parts of several more, had, or ever they began to mount the breach, been blown to pieces by the explosion of a mine, he cried aloud in bitterness, "Would God that my fear had not been discovered before I reached that spot!" But surely it is better to pass into the next region of life having reaped some assurance, some firmness of character, determination of effort, and consciousness of the worth of life, in the present world; so approaching the future steadily and faithfully, and if in much darkness and ignorance, yet not in the oscillations of moral uncertainty.

Close upon the catastrophe followed a torpor, which lasted he did not know how long, and which wrapped in a thick fog all the succeeding events. For some time he can hardly be said to have had any conscious history. He awoke to life and torture when half-way across the sea towards his native country, where was no home any longer for him. To this point, and no farther, could his thoughts return in after years. But the misery which he then endured is hardly to be understood, save by those of like delicate temperament with himself. All day long he sat silent in his cabin; nor could any effort of the captain, or others on board, induce him to go on deck till night came on, when, under the starlight, he ventured into the open air. The sky soothed him then, he knew not how. For the face of nature is the face of God, and must bear expressions that can influence, though unconsciously to them, the most ignorant and hopeless of His children. Often did he watch the clouds in hope of a storm, his spirit rising and falling as the sky darkened or cleared; he longed, in the necessary selfishness of such suffering, for a tumult of waters to swallow the vessel; and only the recollection of how many lives were involved in its safety besides his own, prevented him from praying to God for lightning and tempest, borne on which he might dash into the haven of the other world. One night, following a sultry calm day, he thought that Mercy had heard his unuttered prayer. The air and sea were intense darkness, till a light as intense for one moment annihilated it, and the succeeding darkness seemed shattered with the sharp reports of the thunder that cracked without reverberation. He who had shrunk from battle with his fellowmen, rushed to the mainmast, threw himself on his knees, and stretched forth his arms in speechless energy of supplication; but the storm passed away overhead, and left him kneeling still by the uninjured mast. At length the vessel reached her port. He hurried on shore to bury himself in the most secret place he could find. *Out of sight* was his first, his only thought. Return to his mother he would not, he could not; and, indeed, his friends never learned his fate, until it had carried him far beyond their reach.

For several weeks he lurked about like a malefactor, in low lodging-houses in narrow streets of the seaport to which the vessel had borne him, heeding no one, and but little shocked at the strange society and conversation with which, though only in bodily presence, he had to mingle. These formed the subjects of reflection in after times; and he came to the conclusion that, though much evil and much misery exist, sufficient to move prayers and tears in those who love their kind, yet there is less of both than those looking down from a more elevated social position upon the weltering heap of humanity, are ready to imagine; especially if they regard it likewise from the pedestal of self-congratulation on which a meagre type of religion has elevated them. But at length his little stock of money was nearly expended, and there was nothing that he could do, or learn to do, in this seaport. He felt impelled to seek manual labour, partly because he thought it more likely he could obtain that sort of employment, without a request for reference as to his character, which would lead to inquiry about his previous history; and partly, perhaps, from an instinctive feeling that hard bodily labour would tend to lessen his inward suffering.

He left the town, therefore, at nightfall of a July day, carrying a little bundle of linen, and the remains of his money, somewhat augmented by the sale of various articles of clothing and convenience, which his change of life rendered superfluous and unsuitable. He directed his course northwards, travelling principally by night—so painfully did he shrink from the gaze even of footfarers like himself; and sleeping during the day in some hidden nook of wood or thicket, or under the shadow of a great tree in a solitary field. So fine was the season, that for three successive weeks he was able to travel thus without inconvenience, lying down when the sun grew hot in the forenoon, and generally waking when the first faint stars were hesitating in the great darkening heavens that covered and shielded him. For above every cloud, above every storm, rise up, calm, clear, divine, the deep infinite skies; they embrace the tempest even as the sunshine; by their permission it exists within their boundless peace: therefore it cannot hurt, and must pass away, while there they stand as ever, domed up eternally, lasting, strong, and pure.

Several times he attempted to get agricultural employment; but the whiteness of his hands and the tone of his voice not merely suggested unfitness for labour, but generated suspicion as to the character of one who had evidently dropped from a rank so much higher, and was seeking admittance within the natural masonic boundaries and secrets and privileges of another. Disheartened somewhat, but hopeful, he journeyed on. I say hopeful; for the blessed power of life in the universe, in fresh air and sunshine absorbed by active exercise, in winds, yea in rain, though it fell but seldom, had begun to work its natural healing, soothing effect, upon his perturbed spirit. And there was room for hope in his new endeavour. As his bodily strength increased, and his health, considerably impaired by inward suffering, improved, the trouble of his soul became more endurable—and in some measure to endure is to conquer and destroy. In proportion as the mind grows in the strength of patience, the disturber of its peace sickens and fades away. At length, one day, a widow lady in a village through which his road led him, gave him a day's work in her garden. He laboured hard and well, notwithstanding his soon-blistered hands, received his wages thankfully, and found a resting-place for the night on the low part of a hay-stack from which the upper portion had been cut away. Here he ate his supper of bread and cheese, pleased to have found such comfortable quarters, and soon fell fast asleep.

When he awoke, the whole heavens and earth seemed to give a full denial to sin and sorrow. The sun was just mounting over the horizon, looking up the clear, cloud-mottled sky. From millions of water-drops hanging on the bending stalks of grass, sparkled his rays in varied refraction, transformed here to a gorgeous burning ruby, there to an emerald, green as the grass, and yonder to a flashing, sunny topaz. The chanting priest-lark had gone up from the low earth, as soon as the heavenly light had begun to enwrap and illumine the folds of its tabernacle; and had entered the high heavens with his offering, whence, unseen, he now dropped on the earth the sprinkled sounds of his overflowing blessedness. The poor youth rose but to kneel, and cry, from a bursting heart, "Hast Thou not, O Father, some care for me? Canst Thou not restore my lost honour? Can anything befall Thy children for which Thou hast no help? Surely, if the face of Thy world lie not, joy and not grief is at the heart of the universe. is there none for me?"

The highest poetic feeling of which we are now conscious, springs not from the beholding of perfected beauty, but from the mute sympathy which the creation with all its children manifests with us in the groaning and travailing which look for the sonship. Because of our need and aspiration, the snowdrop gives birth in our hearts to a loftier spiritual and poetic feeling, than the rose most complete in form,

65

colour, and odour. The rose is of Paradise—the snowdrop is of the striving, hoping, longing Earth. Perhaps our highest poetry is the expression of our aspirations in the sympathetic forms of visible nature. Nor is this merely a longing for a restored Paradise; for even in the ordinary history of men, no man or woman that has fallen, can be restored to the position formerly held. Such must rise to a yet higher place, whence they can behold their former standing far beneath their feet. They must be restored by the attainment of something better than they ever possessed before, or not at all. If the law be a weariness, we must escape it by taking refuge with the spirit, for not otherwise can we fulfil the law than by being above the law. To escape the overhanging rocks of Sinai, we must climb to its secret top.

"Is thy strait horizon dreary?
Is thy foolish fancy chill?
Change the feet that have grown weary
For the wings that never will."

Thus, like one of the wandering knights searching the wide earth for the Sangreal, did he wander on, searching for his lost honour, or rather (for that he counted gone for ever) seeking unconsciously for the peace of mind which had departed from him, and taken with it, not the joy merely, but almost the possibility, of existence.

At last, when his little store was all but exhausted, he was employed by a market gardener, in the neighbourhood of a large country town, to work in his garden, and sometimes take his vegetables to market. With him he continued for a few weeks, and wished for no change; until, one day driving his cart through the town, he saw approaching him an elderly gentleman, whom he knew at once, by his gait and carriage, to be a military man. Now he had never seen his uncle the retired officer, but it struck him that this might be he; and under the tyranny of his passion for concealment, he fancied that, if it were he, he might recognise him by some family likeness—not considering the improbability of his looking at him. This fancy, with the painful effect which the sight of an officer, even in plain clothes, had upon him, recalling the torture of that frightful day, so overcame him, that he found himself at the other end of an alley before he recollected that he had the horse and cart in charge. This increased his difficulty; for now he dared not return, lest his inquiries after the vehicle, if the horse had strayed from the direct line, should attract attention, and cause interrogations which he would be unable to answer. The fatal want of self-possession seemed again to ruin him. He forsook the town by the nearest way, struck across the country to another line of road, and before he was missed, was miles away, still in a northerly direction.

But although he thus shunned the face of man, especially of any one who reminded him of the past, the loss of his reputation in their eyes was not the cause of his inward grief. That would have been comparatively powerless to disturb him, had he not lost his own respect. He quailed before his own thoughts; he was dishonoured in his own eyes. His perplexity had not yet sufficiently cleared away to allow him to see the extenuating circumstances of the case; not to say the fact that the peculiar mental condition in which he was at the time, removed the case quite out of the class of ordinary instances of cowardice. He condemned himself more severely than any of his judges would have dared; remembering that portion of his mental sensations which had savoured of fear, and forgetting the causes which had produced it. He judged himself a man stained with the foulest blot that could cleave to a soldier's name, a blot which nothing but death, not even death, could efface. But, inwardly condemned and outwardly degraded, his dread of recognition was intense; and feeling that he was in more danger of being discovered where the population was sparser, he resolved to hide himself once more in the midst of poverty; and, with this view, found his way to one of the largest of the manufacturing towns.

He reached it during the strike of a great part of the workmen; so that, though he found some difficulty in procuring employment, as might be expected from his ignorance of machine-labour, he yet was sooner successful than he would otherwise have been. Possessed of a natural aptitude for mechanical operations, he soon became a tolerable workman; and he found that his previous education assisted to the fitting execution of those operations even which were most purely mechanical.

He found also, at first, that the unrelaxing attention requisite for the mastering of the many niceties of his work, of necessity drew his mind somewhat from its brooding over his misfortune, hitherto almost ceaseless. Every now and then, however, a pang would shoot suddenly to his heart, and turn his face pale, even before his consciousness had time to inquire what was the matter. So by degress, as attention became less necessary, and the nervo-mechanical action of his system increased with use, his thoughts again returned to their old misery. He would wake at night in his poor room, with the feeling that a ghostly nightmare sat on his soul; that a want—a loss—miserable, fearful—was present; that something of his heart was gone from him; and through the darkness he would hear the snap of the breaking sword, and lie for a moment overwhelmed beneath the assurance of the incredible fact. Could it be true that *he* was a

Though the darkness
he would hear the snap of the breaking sword.

coward? that *his* honour was gone, and in its place
a stain? that *he* was a thing for men—and worse, for
women—to point the finger at, laughing bitter laughter? Never lover or husband could have mourned with
the same desolation over the departure of the loved;
the girl alone, weeping scorching tears over *her* degradation, could resemble him in his agony, as he lay
on his bed, and wept and moaned.

His sufferings had returned with the greater weight,
that he was no longer upheld by the "divine air" and
the open heavens, whose sunlight now only reached
him late in an afternoon, as he stood at his loom,
through windows so coated with dust that they looked
like frosted glass; showing, as it passed through the
air to fall on the dirty floor, how the breath of life was
thick with dust of iron and wood, and films of cotton;
amidst which his senses were now too much dulled
by custom to detect the exhalations from greasy
wheels and overtasked human-kind. Nor could he
find comfort in the society of his fellow-labourers.
True, it was a kind of comfort to have those near him
who could not know of his grief; but there was so
little in common between them, that any interchange
of thought was impossible. At least, so it seemed to
him. Yet sometimes his longing for human compan-
ionship would drive him out of his dreary room at
night, and send him wandering through the lower
part of the town, where he would gaze wistfully on
the miserable faces that passed him, as if looking for
some one—some angel, even there—to speak good-
will to his hungry heart.

Once he entered one of those gin-palaces, which,
like the golden gates of hell, entice the miserable to
worse misery, and seated himself close to a half-tipsy,
good-natured wretch, who made room for him on a
bench by the wall. He was comforted even by this
proximity to one who would not repel him. But soon

the paintings of warlike action—of knights, and horses, and mighty deeds done with battle-axe, and broad-sword, which adorned the panels all round, drove him forth even from this heaven of the damned; yet not before the impious thought had arisen in his heart, that the brilliantly painted and sculptural roof, with the gilded vine-leaves and bunches of grapes trained up the windows, all lighted with the great shining chandeliers, was only a microcosmic repetition of the bright heavens and the glowing earth, that overhung and surrounded the misery of man. But the memory of how kindly they had comforted and elevated him, at one period of his painful history, not only banished the wicked thought, but brought him more quiet, in the resurrection of a past blessing, than he had known for some time. The period, however, was now at hand when a new grief, followed by a new and more elevated activity, was to do its part towards the closing up of the fountain of bitterness.

Amongst his fellow-labourers, he had for a short time taken some interest in observing a young woman, who had lately joined them. There was nothing remarkable about her, except what at first sight seemed a remarkable plainness. A slight scar over one of her rather prominent eyebrows, increased this impression of plainness. But the first day had not passed, before he began to see that there was something not altogether common in those deep eyes; and the plain look vanished before a closer observation, which also discovered, in the forehead and the lines of the mouth, traces of sorrow or other suffering. There was an expression, too, in the whole face, of fixedness of purpose, without any hardness of determination. Her countenance altogether seemed the index to an interesting mental history. Signs of mental trouble were always an attraction to him; in this case so great, that he overcame his shyness, and spoke to her one evening as they left the works. He often walked home with her after that; as, indeed, was natural, seeing that she occupied an attic in the same poor lodging-house in which he lived himself. The street did not bear the best character; nor, indeed, would the oc-cupations of all the inmates of the house have stood investigation; but so retiring and quiet was this girl, and so seldom did she go abroad after work hours, that he had not discovered till then that she lived in the same street, not to say the same house, with himself.

He soon learned her history—a very common one as outward events, but not surely insignificant be-cause common. Her father and mother were both dead, and hence she had to find her livelihood alone, and amidst associations which were always disagree-able, and sometimes painful. Her quick womanly in-stinct must have discovered that he too had a history; for though, his mental prostration favouring the op-eration of outward influences, he had greatly approx-imated in appearance to those amongst whom he laboured, there were yet signs, besides the educated accent of his speech, which would have distinguished him to an observer; but she put no questions to him, nor made any approach towards seeking a return of the confidence she reposed in him. It was a sensible alleviation to his sufferings to hear her kind voice, and look in her gentle face, as they walked home to-gether; and at length the expectation of this pleasure began to present itself, in the midst of the busy, dreary work-hours, as the shadow of a heaven to close up the dismal, uninteresting day.

But one morning he missed her from her place, and a keener pain passed through him than he had felt of late; for he knew that the Plague was abroad, feeding in the low stagnant places of human abode; and he had but too much reason to dread that she might be now struggling in its grasp. He seized the first opportunity of slipping out and hurrying home. He sprang upstairs to her room. He found the door locked, but heard a faint moaning within. To avoid disturbing her, while determined to gain an entrance, he went down for the key of his own door, with which he succeeded in unlocking hers, and so crossed her threshold for the first time. There she lay on her bed, tossing in pain, and beginning to be delirious. Careless of his own life, and feeling that he could not die better than in helping the only friend he had; certain, likewise, of the difficulty of finding a nurse for one in this disease and of her station in life; and sure, likewise, that there could be no question of propriety, either in the circumstances with which they were surrounded, nor in this case of terrible fever almost as hopeless for her as dangerous to him, he instantly began the duties of a nurse, and returned no more to his employment. He had a little money in his possession, for he could not, in the way in which he lived, spend all his wages; so he proceeded to make her as comfortable as he could, with all the pent-up tenderness of a loving heart finding an outlet at length. When a boy at home, he had often taken the place of nurse, and he felt quite capable of performing its duties. Nor was his boyhood far behind yet, although the trials he had come through made it appear an age since he had lost his light heart. So he never left her bedside, except to procure what was necessary for her. She was too ill to oppose any of his measures, or to seek to prohibit his presence. Indeed, by the time he had returned with the first medicine, she was insensible; and she continued so through the whole of the following week, during which time he was constantly with her.

That action produces feeling is as often true as its converse; and it is not surprising that, while he smoothed the pillow for her head, he should have made a nest in his heart for the helpless girl. Slowly and unconsciously he learned to love her. The chasm between his early associations and the circumstances in which he found her, vanished as he drew near to the simple, essential womanhood. His heart saw hers and loved it; and he knew that, the centre once gained, he could, as from the fountain of life, as from the innermost secret of the holy place, the hidden germ of power and possibility, transform the outer intellect and outermost manners as he pleased. With what a thrill of joy, a feeling for a long time unknown to him, and till now never known in this form or with this intensity, the thought arose in his heart that here lay one who some day would love him; that he should have a place of refuge and rest; one to lie in his bosom and not despise him! "For," said he to himself, "I will call forth her soul from where it sleeps, like an una-wakened echo, in an unknown cave; and like a child, of whom I once dreamed, that was mine, and to my delight turned in fear from all besides, and clung to me, this soul of hers will run with bewildered, half-sleeping eyes, and tottering steps, but with a cry of joy on its lips, to me as the life-giver. She will cling to me and worship me. Then will I tell her, for she must know all, that I am low and contemptible; that I am an outcast from the world, and that if she receive me, she will be to me as God. And I will fall down at her feet and pray her for comfort, for life, for resto-ration to myself; and she will throw herself beside me, and weep and love me, I know. And we will go through life together, working hard, but for each other; and when we die, she shall lead me into paradise as the prize her angel-hand found cast on a desert shore, from the storm of winds and waves which I was too weak to resist—and raised, and tended, and saved." Often did such thoughts as these pass through his mind while watching her bed; alternated, checked, and sometimes destroyed, by the fears which attended her precarious condition, but returning with every apparent betterment or hopeful symptom.

I will not stop to decide the nice question, how far the intention was right, of causing her to love him before she knew his story. If in the whole matter there was too much thought of self, my only apology is the sequel. One day, the ninth from the commencement of her illness, a letter arrived, addressed to her; which he, thinking he might prevent some inconvenience thereby, opened and read, in the confidence of that love which already made her and all belonging to her appear his own. It was from a soldier—*her lover*. It was plain that they had been betrothed before he left for the continent a year ago; but this was the first letter which he had written to her. It breathed changeless love, and hope, and confidence in her. He was so fascinated that he read it through without pause.

Laying it down, he sat pale, motionless, almost inanimate. From the hard-won sunny heights, he was once more cast down into the shadow of death. The second storm of his life began, howling and raging, with yet more awful lulls between. "Is she not *mine*?" he said, in agony. "Do I not feel that she is mine? Who will watch over her as I? Who will kiss her soul to life as I? Shall she be torn away from me, when my soul seems to have dwelt with hers for ever in an eternal house? But have I not a right to her? Have I not given my life for hers? Is he not a soldier, and are there not many chances that he may never return? And it may be that, although they were engaged in word, soul has never touched soul with them; their love has never reached that point where it passes from the mortal to the immortal, the indissoluble: and so, in a sense, she may be yet free. Will he do for her what I will do? Shall this precious heart of hers, in which I see the buds of so many beauties, be left to wither and die?"

But here the voice within him cried out, "Art thou the disposer of destinies? Wilt thou, in a universe where the visible God hath died for the Truth's sake, do evil that a good, which He might neglect or overlook, may be gained? Leave thou her to Him, and do thou right." And he said within himself, "Now is the real trial for my life! Shall I conquer or no?" And his heart awoke and cried, "I will. God forgive me for wronging the poor soldier! A brave man, brave at least, is better for her than I."

A great strength arose within him, and lifted him up to depart. "Surely I may kiss her once," he said. For the crisis was over, and she slept. He stooped towards her face, but before he had reached her lips he saw her eyelids tremble; and he who had longed for the opening of those eyes, as of the gates of heaven, that she might love him, stricken now with fear lest she should love him, fled from her, before the eyelids that hid such strife and such victory from the unconscious maiden had time to unclose. But it was agony—quietly to pack up his bundle of linen in the room below, when he knew she was lying awake above, with her dear, pale face, and living eyes! What remained of his money, except a few shillings, he put up in a scrap of paper, and went out with his bundle in his hand, first to seek a nurse for his friend, and then to go he knew not whither. He met the factory people with whom he had worked, going to dinner, and amongst them a girl who had herself but lately recovered from the fever, and was yet hardly able for work. She was the only friend the sick girl had seemed to have amongst the women at the factory, and she was easily persuaded to go and take charge of her. He put the money in her hand, begging her to use it for the invalid, and promising to send the equivalent of her wages for the time he thought she would have to wait on her. This he easily did by the sale of a ring, which, besides his mother's watch, was the only article of value he had retained. He begged her likewise not to mention his name in the matter; and was foolish enough to expect that she would entirely keep the promise she had made him.

Wandering along the street, purposeless now and bereft, he spied a recruiting party at the door of a public-house; and on coming nearer, found, by one of those strange coincidences which do occur in life, and which have possibly their root in a hidden and wondrous law, that it was a party, perhaps a remnant, of the very regiment in which he had himself served, and in which his misfortune had befallen him. Almost simultaneously with the shock which the sight of the well-known number on the soldiers' knapsacks gave him, arose in his mind the romantic, ideal thought, of enlisting in the ranks of this same regiment, and recovering, as a private soldier and unknown, that honour which as officer he had lost. To this determination, the new necessity in which he now stood for action and change of life, doubtless contributed, though unconsciously. He offered himself to the sergeant; and, notwithstanding that his dress indicated a mode of life unsuitable as the antecedent to a soldier's, his appearance, and the necessity for recruits combined, led to his easy acceptance.

The English armies were employed in expelling the enemy from an invaded and helpless country. Whatever might be the political motives which had induced the government to this measure, the young man was now able to feel that he could go and fight, individually and for his part, in the cause of liberty. He was free to possess his own motives for joining in the execution of the schemes of those who commanded his commanders.

With a heavy heart, but with more of inward hope and strength than he had ever known before, he marched with his comrades to the seaport and embarked. It seemed to him that because he had done right in his last trial, here was a new glorious chance held out to his hand. True, it was a terrible change to pass from a woman in whom he had hoped to find healing, into the society of rough men, to march with the, *"mit gleichem Tritt und Schritt,"* up to the bristling bayonets or the horrid vacancy of the cannon mouth. But it was the only cure for the evil that consumed his life.

He reached the army in safety, and gave himself, with religious assiduity, to the smallest duties of his new position. No one had a brighter polish on his arms, or whiter belts than he. In the necessary movements, he soon became precise to a degree that attracted the attention of his officers; while his character was remarkable for all the virtues belonging to a perfect soldier.

One day, as he stood sentry, he saw the eyes of his colonel intently fixed on him. He felt his lip quiver, but he compressed and stilled it, and tried to look as unconscious as he could; which effort was assisted by the formal bearing required by his position. Now the colonel, such had been the losses of the regiment, had been promoted from a lieutenancy in the same, and had belonged to it at the time of the ensign's degradation. Indeed, had not the changes in the regiment been so great, he could hardly have escaped so long without discovery. But the poor fellow would have felt that his name was already free of reproach, if he had seen what followed on the close inspection which had awakened his apprehensions, and which, in fact, had convinced the colonel of his identity with the disgraced ensign. With a hasty and less soldierly step than usual, the colonel entered his tent, threw himself on his bed, and wept like a child. When he rose he was overheard to say these words—and these only escaped his lips: "He is nobler than I."

But this officer showed himself worthy of commanding such men as this private; for right nobly did he understand and meet his feelings. He uttered no word of the discovery he had made, till years afterwards; but it soon began to be remarked that whenever anything arduous, or in any manner distinguished, had to be done, this man was sure to be of the party appointed. In short, as often as he could, the colonel "set him in the forefront of the battle." Passing through all with wonderful escape, he was soon as much noticed for his reckless bravery, as hitherto for his precision in the discharge of duties, bringing only commendation and not honour. But his final lustration was at hand.

A great part of the army was hastening, by forced marches, to raise the siege of a town which was already on the point of falling into the hands of the enemy. Forming one of a reconnoitring party, which preceded the main body at some considerable distance, he and his companions came suddenly upon one of the enemy's outposts, occupying a high, and on one side precipitous rock, a short way from the town, which it commanded. Retreat was impossible, for they were already discovered, and the bullets were falling amongst them like the first of a hail-storm. The only possibility of escape remaining for them was a nearby hopeless improbability. It lay in forcing the post on this steep rock; which if they could do before assistance came to the enemy, they might, perhaps, be able to hold out, by means of its defences, till the arrival of the army. Their position was at once understood by all; and, by a sudden, simultaneous impulse, they found themselves halfway up the steep ascent, and in the struggle of a close conflict, without being aware of any order to that effect from their officer. But their courage was of no avail; the advantages of the place were too great; and in a few minutes the whole party was cut to pieces, or stretched helpless on the rock. Our youth had fallen amongst the foremost; for a musket ball had grazed his skull, and laid him insensible.

But consciousness slowly returned, and he succeeded at last in raising himself and looking around him. The place was deserted. A few of his friends, alive, but grievously wounded, lay near him. The rest were dead. It appeared that, learning the proximity of the English forces from this rencontre with part of their advanced guard, and dreading lest the town, which was on the point of surrendering, should after all be snatched from their grasp, the commander of the enemy's forces had ordered an immediate and general assault; and had for this purpose recalled from their outposts the whole of his troops thus stationed, that he might make the attempt with the utmost strength he could accumulate.

As the youth's power of vision returned, he perceived, from the height where he lay, that the town was already in the hands of the enemy. But looking down into the level space immediately below him, he started to his feet at once; for a girl, bare-headed, was fleeing towards the rock, pursued by several soldiers. "Aha!" said he, divining her purpose—the soldiers behind and the rock before her—"I will help you to die!" And he stooped and wrenched from the dead fingers of a sergeant the sword which they clenched by the bloody hilt. A new throb of life pulsed through him to his very finger-tips; and on the brink of the unseen world he stood, with the blood rushing through his veins in a wild dance of excitement. One who lay near him wounded, but recovered afterwards, said that he looked like one inspired. With a keen eye he watched the chase. The girl drew nigh; and rushed up the path near which he was standing. Close on her footsteps came the soldiers, the distance gradually lessening between them.

Not many paces higher up, was a narrower part of the ascent, where the path was confined by great stones, or pieces of rock. Here had been the chief defence in the preceding assault, and in it lay many bodies of his friends. Thither he went and took his stand.

On the girl came, over the dead, with rigid hands and flying feet, the bloodless skin drawn tight on her features, and her eyes awfully large and wild. She did not see him though she bounded past so near that her hair flew in his eyes. "Never mind!" said he, "we shall meet soon." And he stepped into the narrow path just in time to face her pursuers—between her and them. Like the red lightning, the bloody sword fell, and a man beneath it. Cling! clang! went the echoes in the rocks—and another man was down; for, in his excitement, he was destroying angel to the breathless pursuers. His stature rose, his chest dilated; and as the third foe fell dead, the girl was safe; for her body lay a broken, empty, but undesecrated temple, at the foot of the rock. That moment his sword flew in shivers from his grasp. The next instant he fell, pierced to the heart; and his spirit rose triumphant, free, strong, and calm, above the stormy world, which at length lay vanquished beneath him.

THE WOW O' RIVVEN
The Bell

ELSIE Scott had let her work fall on her knees, and her hands on her work, and was looking out of the wide, low window of her room, which was on one of the ground floors of the village street. Through a gap in the household shrubbery of fuchsias and myrtles filling the window-sill, one passing on the foot-pavement might get a momentary glimpse of her pale face, lighted up with two blue eyes, over which some inward trouble had spread a faint, gauze-like haziness. But almost before her thoughts had had time to wander back to this trouble, a shout of children's voices, at the other end of the street, reached her ear. She listened a moment. A shadow of displeasure and pain crossed her countenance; and rising hastily, she betook herself to an inner apartment, and closed the door behind her.

Meantime the sounds drew nearer; and by and by, an old man, whose strange appearance and dress showed that he had little capacity either for good or evil, passed the window. His clothes were comfortable enough in quality and condition, for they were the annual gift of a benevolent lady in the neighbourhood; but, being made to accommodate his taste,

First appeared as "The Bell" in *Good Words* (1864); reprinted in *Adela Cathcart* (1864).

both known and traditional, they were somewhat peculiar in cut and adornment. Both coat and trousers were of a dark grey cloth; but the former, which, in its shape, partook of the military, had a straight collar of yellow, and narrow cuffs of the same; while upon both sleeves, about the place where a corporal wears his stripes, was expressed, in the same yellow cloth, a somewhat singular device. It was as close an imitation of a bell, with its tongue hanging out of its mouth, as the tailor's skill could produce from a single piece of cloth. The origin of the military cut of his coat was well known. His preference for it arose in the time of the wars of the first Napoleon, when the threatened invasion of the country caused the organization of many volunteer regiments. The martial show and exercises captivated the poor man's fancy; and from that time forward nothing pleased his vanity, and consequently conciliated his good-will more, than to style him by his favourite title—the *Colonel*. But the badge on his arm had a deeper origin, which will be partially manifest in the course of the story— if story it can be called. It was, indeed, the baptism of the fool, the outward and visible sign of his relation to the infinite and unseen. His countenance, however, although the features were not of any peculiarly low or animal type, showed no corresponding sign of the consciousness of such a relation, being as vacant as human countenance could well be.

The cause of Elsie's annoyance was that the fool was annoyed; he was followed by a troop of boys, who turned his rank into scorn, and assailed him with epithets hateful to him. Although the most harmless of creatures when let alone, he was dangerous when roused; and now he stooped repeatedly to pick up stones and hurl them at his tormentors, who took care, while abusing him, to keep at a considerable distance, lest he should get hold of them.

GEORGE MACDONALD

Amidst the sounds of derision that followed him, might be heard the words frequently repeated—*"Come hame, come hame."* But in a few minutes the noise ceased, either from the interference of some friendly inhabitant, or that the boys grew weary, and departed in search of other amusement. By and by, Elsie might be seen again at her work in the window; but the cloud over her eyes was deeper, and her whole face more sad.

Indeed, so much did the persecution of this poor man affect her, that an onlooker would have been compelled to seek the cause in some yet deeper sympathy than that commonly felt for the oppressed, even by women. And such a sympathy existed, strange as it may seem, between the beautiful girl (for many called her *a bonnie lassie*) and this "tatter of humanity." Nothing would have been further from the thoughts of those that knew them, than the supposition of any correspondence or connexion between them; yet this sympathy sprang in part from a real similarity in their history and present condition.

All the facts that were known about *Feel Jock's* origin were these: that seventy years ago, a man who had gone with his horse and cart some miles from the village, to fetch home a load of peat from a desolate *moss*, had heard, while toiling along as rough a road on as lonely a hill-side as any in Scotland, the cry of a child; and, searching about, had found the infant, hardly wrapt in rags, and untended, as if the earth herself had just given him birth,—that desert moor, wide and dismal, broken and watery, the only bosom for him to lie upon, and the cold, clear night-heaven his only covering. The man had brought him home, and the parish had taken parish-care of him. He had grown up, and proved what he now was— almost an idiot. Many of the townspeople were kind to him, and employed him in fetching water for them

84

from the river or wells in the neighbourhood, paying him for his trouble in victuals, or whisky, of which he was very fond. He seldom spoke; and the sentences he could utter were few; yet the tone, and even the words of his limited vocabulary, were sufficient to express gratitude and some measure of love towards those who were kind to him, and hatred of those who teased and insulted him. He lived a life without aim, and apparently to no purpose; in this resembling most of his more gifted fellow-men, who, with all the tools and materials necessary for building a noble mansion, are yet content with a clay hut.

Elsie, on the contrary, had been born in a comfortable farm-house, amidst homeliness and abundance. But at a very early age, she had lost both father and mother; not so early, however, but that she had faint memories of warm soft times on her mother's bosom, and of refuge in her mother's arms from the attacks of geese, and the pursuit of pigs. Therefore, in after-times, when she looked forward to heaven, it was as much a reverting to the old heavenly times of childhood and mother's love, as an anticipation of something yet to be revealed. Indeed, without some such memory, how should we ever picture to ourselves a perfect rest? But sometimes it would seem as if the more a heart was made capable of loving, the less it had to love; and poor Elsie, in passing from a mother's to a brother's guardianship, felt a change of spiritual temperature too keen. He was not a bad man, or incapable of benevolence when touched by the sight of want in anything of which he would himself have felt the privation; but he was so coarsely made, that only the purest animal necessities affected him; and a hard word, or unfeeling speech, could never have reached the quick of his nature through the hide that enclosed it. Elsie, on the contrary, was excessively and painfully sensitive, as if her nature constantly portended an invisible multitude of half-spiritual, half-nervous antennae, which shrank and trembled in every current of air at all below their own temperature. The effect of this upon her behaviour was such, that she was called odd; and the poor girl felt she was not like other people, yet could not help it. Her brother, too, laughed at her without the slightest idea of the pain he occasioned, or the remotest feeling of curiosity as to what the inward and consistent causes of the outward abnormal condition might be. Tenderness was the divine comforting she needed; and it was altogether absent from her brother's character and behaviour.

Her neighbours looked on her with some interest, but they rather shunned than courted her acquaintance; especially after the return of certain nervous attacks, to which she had been subject in childhood, and which were again brought on by the events I must relate. It is curious how certain diseases repel, by a kind of awe, the sympathies of the neighbours: as if, by the fact of being subject to them, the patient were removed into another realm of existence, from which, like the dead with the living, she can hold communion with those around her only partially, and with a mixture of dread pervading the intercourse. Thus some of the deepest, purest wells of spiritual life, are, like those in old castles, choked up by the decay of the outer walls. But what tended more than anything, perhaps, to keep up the painful unrest of her soul (for the beauty of her character was evident in the fact, that the irritation seldom reached her *mind*), was a circumstance at which, in its present connexion, some of my readers will smile, and others feel a shudder corresponding in kind to that of Elsie.

Her brother was very fond of a rather small, but ferocious-looking bull-dog, which followed close at his heels, wherever he went, with hanging head and

slouching gait, never leaping or racing about like other
dogs. When in the house, he always lay under his
master's chair. He seemed to dislike Elsie, and she
felt an unspeakable repugnance to him. Though she
never mentioned her aversion, her brother easily saw
it by the way in which she avoided the animal; and
attributing it entirely to fear—which indeed had a
great share in the matter—he would cruelly aggravate
it, by telling her stories of the fierce hardihood and
relentless persistency of this kind of animal. He dared
not yet further increase her terror by offering to set
the creature upon her, because it was doubtful
whether he might be able to restrain him; but the
mental suffering which he occasioned by this heart-
less conduct, and for which he had no sympathy, was
as severe as many bodily sufferings to which he would
have been sorry to subject her. Whenever the poor
girl happened inadvertently to pass near the dog,
which was seldom, a low growl made her aware of
his proximity, and drove her to a quick retreat. He
was, in fact, the animal impersonation of the animal
opposition which she had continually to endure. Like
chooses like; and the bull-dog *in* her brother made
choice of the bull-dog *out of* him for his companion.
So her day was one of shrinking fear and multiform
discomfort.

But a nature capable of so much distress, must of
necessity be *capable* of a corresponding amount of
pleasure; and in her case this was manifest in the
fact, that sleep and the quiet of her own room restored her wonderfully. If she was only let alone, a
calm mood, filled with images of pleasure, soon took
possession of her mind.

Her acquaintance with the fool had commenced
some ten years previous to the time I write of, when
she was quite a little girl, and had come from the
country with her brother, who, having taken a small

farm close to the town, preferred residing in the town to occupying the farm-house, which was not comfortable. She looked at first with some terror on his uncouth appearance, and with much wonderment on his strange dress. This wonder was heightened by a conversation she overheard one day in the street, between the fool and a little pale-faced boy, who, approaching him respectfully, said, "Weel, cornel!" "Weel, laddie!" was the reply. "Fat dis the wow say, cornel?" "Come hame, come hame!" answered the *colonel*, with both accent and quantity heaped on the word *hame*. What the *wow* could be, she had no idea; only, as the years passed on, the strange word became in her mind indescribably associated with the strange shape in yellow cloth on his sleeves. Had she been a native of the town, she could not have failed to know its import, so familiar was every one with it, although it did not belong to the local vocabulary; but, as it was, years passed away before she discovered its meaning. And when, again and again, the fool, attempting to convey his gratitude for some kindness she had shown him, mumbled over the words—*The wow o' Rivven—the wow o' Rivven*," the wonder would return as to what could be the idea associated with them in his mind, but she made no advance towards their explanation.

That, however, which most attracted her to the old man, was his persecution by the children. They were to him what the bull-dog was to her—the constant source of irritation and annoyance. They could hardly hurt him, nor did he appear to dread other injury from them than insult, to which, fool though he was, he was keenly alive. Human gad-flies that they were! they sometimes stung him beyond endurance, and he would curse them in the impotence of his anger. Once or twice Elsie had been so far carried beyond her constitutional timidity, by sympathy for the distress of her friend, that she had gone out and talked to the boys,—even scolded them, so that they slunk away ashamed, and began to stand as much in dread of her as of the clutches of their prey. So she, gentle and timid to excess, acquired among them the reputation of a termagant.* Popular opinion among children, as among men, is often just, but as often very unjust; for the same manifestations may proceed from opposite principles; and, therefore, as indices to character, may mislead as often as enlighten.

Next door to the house in which Elsie resided, dwelt a tradesman and his wife, who kept an indefinite sort of shop, in which various kinds of goods were exposed for sale. Their youngest son was about the same age as Elsie; and while they were rather more than children, and less than young people, he spent many of his evenings with her, somewhat to the loss of position in his classes at the parish school. They were, indeed, much attached to each other; and, peculiarly constituted as Elsie was, one may imagine what kind of heavenly messenger a companion stronger than herself must have been to her. In fact, if she could have framed the undefinable need of her child-like nature into an articulate prayer, it would have been—"Give me some one to love me stronger than I." Any love was helpful, yes, in its degree, saving to her poor troubled soul; but the hope, as they grew older together, that the powerful, yet tender-hearted youth, really loved her, and would one day make her his wife, was like the opening of heavenly eyes of life and love in the hitherto blank and death-like face of her existence. But nothing had been said of love, although they met and parted like lovers.

Doubtless, if the circles of their thought and feeling had continued as now to intersect each other,

---

*A turbulent girl.

there would have been no interruption to their affection; but the time at length arrived when the old couple, seeing the rest of their family comfortably settled in life, resolved to make a gentleman of the youngest; and so sent him from school to college. The facilities existing in Scotland for providing a professional training enabled them to educate him as a surgeon. He parted from Elsie with some regret; but, far less dependent on her than she was on him, and full of the prospects of the future, he felt none of that sinking at the heart which seemed to lay her whole nature open to a fresh inroad of all the terrors and sorrows of her peculiar existence. No correspondence took place between them. New pursuits and relations, and the development of his tastes and judgments, entirely altered the position of poor Elsie in his memory. Having been, during their intercourse, far less of a man than she of a woman, he had no definite idea of the place he had occupied in her regard; and in his mind she receded into the background of the past, without his having any idea that she would suffer thereby, or that he was unjust towards her; while, in her thoughts, his image stood in the highest and clearest relief. It was the centre-point from which and towards which all lines radiated and converged; and although she could not but be doubtful about the future, yet there was much hope mingled with her doubts.

But when, at the close of two years, he visited his native village, and she saw before her, instead of the homely youth who had left her that winter evening, one who, to her inexperienced eyes, appeared a finished gentleman, her heart sank within her, as if she had found Nature herself false in her ripening processes, destroying the beautiful promise of a former year by changing instead of developing her creations. He spoke kindly to her, but not cordially. To her ear the voice seemed to come from a great distance out of the past; and while she looked upon him, that optical change passed over her vision, which all have experienced after gazing abstractedly on any object for a time: his form grew very small, and receded to an immeasurable distance; till, her imagination mingling with the twilight haze of her senses, she seemed to see him standing far off on a hill, with the bright horizon of sunset for a background to his clearly defined figure.

She knew no more till she found herself in bed in the dark; and the first message that reached her from the outer world, was the infernal growl of the bulldog from the room below. Next day she saw her lover walking with two ladies, who would have thought it some degree of condescension to speak to her; and he passed the house without once looking towards it.

One who is sufficiently possessed by the demon of nervousness to be glad of the magnetic influences of a friend's company in a public promenade, or of a horse beneath him in passing through a churchyard, will have some faint idea of how utterly exposed and defenceless poor Elsie now felt on the crowded thoroughfare of life. And so the insensibility which had overtaken her, was not the ordinary swoon with which Nature relieves the overstrained nerves, but the return of the epileptic fits of her early childhood; and if the condition of the poor girl had been pitiable before, it was tenfold more so now. Yet she did not complain, but bore all in silence, though it was evident that her health was giving way. But now, help came to her from a strange quarter; though many might not be willing to accord the name of help to that which rather hastened than retarded the progress of her decline.

She had gone to spend a few of the summer days with a relative in the country, some miles from her home, if home it could be called. One evening, towards sunset, she went out for a solitary walk. Passing from the little garden-gate, she went along a bare country road for some distance, and then turning aside by a footpath through a thicket of low trees, she came out in a lonely little churchyard on the hill-side. Hardly knowing whether or not she had intended to go there, she seated herself on a mound covered with long grass, one of many. Before her stood the ruins of an old church which was taking centuries to crumble. Little remained but the gable-wall, immensely thick, and covered with ancient ivy. The rays of the setting sun fell on a mound at its foot, not green like the rest, but of a rich, red-brown in the rosy sunset, and evidently but newly heaped up. Her eyes, too, rested upon it. Slowly the sun sank below the near horizon.

As the last brilliant point disappeared, the ivy darkened, and a wind arose and shook all its leaves, making them look cold and troubled; and to Elsie's ear came a low faint sound, as from a far-off bell. But close beside her—and she started and shivered at the sound—rose a deep, monotonous, almost sepulchral voice, *"Come hame, come hame! The wow, the wow!"*

At once she understood the whole. She sat in the churchyard of the ancient parish church of Ruthven; and when she lifted up her eyes, there she saw, in the half-ruined belfry, the old bell, all but hidden with ivy, which the passing wind had roused to utter one sleepy tone; and there, beside her, stood the fool with the bell on his arm; and to him and to her the *wow o' Rivven* said, *"Come hame, come hame!"* Ah, what did she want in the whole universe of God but a home? And though the ground beneath was hard, and the sky overhead far and boundless, and the hill-side lonely and companionless, yet somewhere within the visible, and beyond these the outer surfaces of

Before her stood the ruins
of an old church
which was taking centuries to crumble.

creation, there might be a home for her; as round the
wintry house the snows lie heaped up cold and white
and dreary all the long *forenight*, while within, beyond the closed shutters, and giving no glimmer
through the thick stone walls, the fires are blazing
joyously, and the voices and laughter of young un-
frozen children are heard, and nothing belongs to
winter but the grey hairs on the heads of the parents,
within whose warm hearts child-like voices are heard,
and child-like thoughts move to and fro. The kernel
of winter itself is spring, or a sleeping summer.

It was no wonder that the fool, cast out of the
earth on a far more desolate spot than this, should
seek to return within her bosom at this place of open
doors, and should call it *home*. For surely the surface
of the earth had no home for him. The mound at the
foot of the gable contained the body of one who had
shown him kindness. He had followed the funeral
that afternoon from the town, and had remained behind with the bell. Indeed, it was his custom, though
Elsie had not known it, to follow every funeral going
to this, his favourite churchyard of Ruthven; and,
possibly in imitation of its booming, for it was still
tolled at the funerals, he had given the old bell the
name of *the wow*, and had translated its monotonous
clangour into the articulate sounds—*come hame, come
hame*. What precise meaning he attached to the words,
it is impossible to say; but it was evident that the
place possessed a strange attraction for him, drawing
him towards it by the cords of some spiritual mag-
netism. It is possible that in the mind of the idiot
there may have been some feeling about this churchyard and bell, which, in the mind of another, would
have become a grand poetic thought; a feeling as if
the ghostly old bell hung at the church-door of the
invisible world, and ever and anon rang out joyous
notes (though they sounded sad in the ears of the

living), calling to the children of the unseen to *come home, come home*. She sat for some time in silence; for the bell did not ring again, and the fool spoke no more; till the dews began to fall, when she rose and went home, followed by her companion, who passed the night in the barn.

From that hour Elsie was furnished with a visual image of the rest she sought; an image which, mingling with deeper and holier thoughts, became, like the bow set in the cloud, the earthly pledge and sign of the fulfilment of heavenly hopes. Often when the wintry fog of cold discomfort and homelessness filled her soul, all at once the picture of the little churchyard—with the old gable and belfry, and the slanting sunlight steeping down to the very roots of the long grass on the graves—arose in the darkened chamber *(camera obscura)* of her soul; and again she heard the faint Aeolian sound of the bell, and the voice of the prophet-fool who interpreted the oracle; and the inward weariness was soothed by the promise of a long sleep. Who can tell how many have been counted fools simply because they were prophets; or how much of the madness in the world may be the utterance of thoughts true and just, but belonging to a region differing from ours in its nature and scenery!

But to Elsie looking out of her window came the mocking tones of the idle boys who had chosen as the vehicle of their scorn the very words which showed the relation of the fool to the eternal, and revealed in him an element higher far than any yet developed in them. They turned his glory into shame, like the enemies of David when they mocked the would-be king. And the best in a man is often that which is most condemned by those who have not attained to his goodness. The words, however, even as repeated by the boys, had not solely awakened indignation at the persecution of the old man: they had likewise comforted her with the thought of the refuge that awaited both him and her.

But the same evening a worse trial was in store for her. Again she sat near the window, oppressed by the consciousness that her brother had come in. He had gone up-stairs, and his dog had remained at the door, exchanging surly compliments with some of his own kind, when the fool came strolling past, and, I do not know from what cause, the dog flew at him. Elsie heard his cry and looked up. Her fear of the brute vanished in a moment before her sympathy for her friend. She darted from the house, and rushed towards the dog to drag him off the defenceless idiot, calling him by his name in a tone of anger and dislike. He left the fool, and, springing at Elsie, seized her by the arm above the elbow with such a grip that, in the midst of her agony, she fancied she heard the bone crack. But she uttered no cry, for the most apprehensive are sometimes the most courageous. Just then, however, her former lover was coming along the street, and, catching a glimpse of what had happened, was on the spot in an instant, took the dog by the throat with a grip not inferior to his own, and having thus compelled him to relax his hold, dashed him on the ground with a force that almost stunned him, and then with a superadded kick sent him away limping and howling; whereupon the fool, attacking him furiously with a stick, would certainly have finished him, had not his master descried his plight and come to his rescue.

Meantime the young surgeon had carried Elsie into the house; for, as soon as she was rescued from the dog, she had fallen down in one of her fits, which were becoming more and more frequent of themselves, and little needed such a shock as this to increase their violence. He was dressing her arm when she began to recover; and when she opened her eyes, in a state of half-consciousness, the first object she beheld, was his face bending over her. Recalling nothing of what had occurred, it seemed to her, in the dreamy condition in which the fit had left her, the same face, unchanged, which had once shone in upon her tardy spring-time, and promised to ripen it into summer. She forgot it had departed and left her in the wintry cold. And so she uttered wild words of love and trust; and the youth, while stung with remorse at his own neglect, was astonished to perceive the poetic forms of beauty in which the soul of the uneducated maiden burst into flower. But as her senses recovered themselves, the face gradually changed to her, as if the slow alteration of two years had been phantasmagorically compressed into a few moments; and the glow departed from the maiden's thoughts and words, and her soul found itself at the narrow window of the present, from which she could behold but a dreary country. —From the street came the iambic cry of the fool, *"Come hame, come hame."*

Tycho Brahe, I think, is said to have kept a fool, who frequently sat at his feet in his study, and to whose mutterings he used to listen in the pauses of his own thought. The shining soul of the astronomer drew forth the rainbow of harmony from the misty spray of words ascending ever from the dark gulf into which the thoughts of the idiot were ever falling. He beheld curious concurrences of words therein, and could read strange meanings from them—sometimes even received wondrous hints for the direction of celestial inquiry, from what, to any other, and it may be to the fool himself, was but a ceaseless and aimless babble. Such power lieth in words. It is not then to be wondered at, that the sounds I have mentioned should fall on the ears of Elsie, at such a moment, as a message from God himself. This then—all this dreariness—was but a passing show like the rest, and there lay somewhere for her a reality—a home. The tears burst up from her oppressed heart. She received the message, and prepared to go home. From that time her strength gradually sank, but her spirits as steadily rose.

The strength of the fool, too, began to fail, for he was old. He bore all the signs of age, even to the grey hairs, which betokened no wisdom. But one cannot say what wisdom might be in him, or how far he had not fought his own battle, and been victorious. Whether any notion of a continuance of life and thought dwelt in his brain, it is impossible to tell; but he seemed to have the idea that this was not his home; and those who saw him gradually approaching his end, might well anticipate for him a higher life in the world to come. He had passed through this world without ever awaking to such a consciousness of being as is common to mankind. He had spent his years like a weary dream through a long night,—a strange, dismal, unkindly dream; and now the morning was at hand. Often in his dream had he listened with sleepy senses to the ringing of the bell, but that bell would awake him at last. He was like a seed buried too deep in the soil, to which the light has never penetrated, and which, therefore, has never forced its way upwards to the open air, never experienced the resurrection of the dead. But seeds will grow ages after they have fallen into the earth; and, indeed, with many kinds, and within some limits, the older seed before it germinates, the more plentiful the fruit. And may it not be believed of many human beings, that, the great Husbandman having sown them like seeds in the soil of human affairs, there they lie buried a life long; and only after the upturning of the soil by death, reach a position in which the awakening of their aspiration and the consequent growth become possible. Surely he has made nothing in vain.

A violent cold and cough brought him at last near to his end, and hearing that he was ill, Elsie ventured one bright spring day to go to see him. When she entered the miserable room where he lay, he held out his hand to her with something like a smile, and muttered feebly and painfully, "I'm gaein' to the wow, nae to come back again." Elsie could not restrain her tears; while the old man, looking fixedly at her, though with meaningless eyes, muttered for the last time, *"Come hame! come hame!"* and sank into a lethargy, from which nothing could rouse him, till, next morning, he was waked by friendly death from the long sleep of this world's night. They bore him to his favourite churchyard, and buried him within the site of the old church, below his loved bell, which had ever been to him as the cuckoo-note of a coming spring. Thus he at length obeyed its summons, and went home.

Elsie lingered till the first summer days lay warm on the land. Several kind hearts in the village, hearing of her illness, visited her and ministered to her. Wondering at her sweetness and patience, they regretted they had not known her before. How much consolation might not their kindness have imparted, and how much might not their sympathy have strengthened her on her painful road! But they could not long have delayed her going home. Nor, mentally constituted as she was, would this have been at all to be desired. Indeed it was chiefly the expectation of departure that quieted and soothed her tremulous nature. It is true that a deep spring of hope and faith kept singing on in her heart, but this alone, without the anticipation of speedy release, could only have kept her mind at peace. It could not have reached, at least for a long time, the border land between body and mind, in which her disease lay.

One still night of summer, the nurse who watched by her bed-side heard her murmur through her sleep, "I hear it: *come hame—come hame.* I'm comin', I'm comin'—I'm gaein' hame to the wow, nae to come back." She awoke at the sound of her own words, and begged the nurse to convey to her brother her last request, that she might be buried by the side of the fool, within the old church of Ruthven. Then she turned her face to the wall, and in the morning was found quiet and cold. She must have died within a few minutes after her last words. She was buried according to her request; and thus she too went home.

Side by side rest the aged fool and the young maiden; for the bell called them and they obeyed; and surely they found the fire burning bright, and heard friendly voices, and felt sweet lips on theirs, in the home to which they went. Surely both intellect and love were waiting them there.

Still the old bell hangs in the old gable; and whenever another is borne to the old churchyard, it keeps calling to those who are left behind, with the same sad, but friendly and unchanging voice—*"Come hame! come hame! come hame!"*

"Thy sun shall no more go down; neither shall thy moon withdraw itself: for the LORD shall be thine everlasting light, and the days of thy mourning shall be ended."—*Isaiah lx. 20.*

UNCLE CORNELIUS, HIS STORY

IT was a dull evening in November. A drizzling mist had been falling all day about the old farm. Harry Heywood and his two sisters sat in the house-place, expecting a visit from their uncle, Cornelius Heywood. This uncle lived alone, occupying the first floor above a chemist's shop in the town, and had just enough of money over to buy books that nobody seemed ever to have heard of but himself; for he was a student in all those regions of speculation in which anything to be called knowledge is impossible.

"What a dreary night!" said Kate. "I wish uncle would come and tell us a story."

"A cheerful wish," said Harry. "Uncle Cornie is a lively companion,—isn't he? He can't even blunder through a Joe Miller without tacking a moral to it, and then trying to persuade you that the joke of it depends on the moral."

"Here he comes!" said Kate, as three distinct blows with the knob of his walking-stick announced the arrival of Uncle Cornelius. She ran to the door to open it.

The air had been very still all day, but as he entered he seemed to have brought the wind with him, for

Reprinted from *Works of Fancy and Imagination* (1871).

the first moan of it pressed against rather than shook the casement of the low-ceiled room.

Uncle Cornelius was very tall, and very thin, and very pale, with large gray eyes that looked greatly larger because he wore spectacles of the most delicate hair-steel, with the largest pebble-eyes that ever were seen. He gave them a kindly greeting, but too much in earnest even in shaking hands to smile over it. He sat down in the armchair by the chimney corner.

I have been particular in my description of him, in order that my reader may give due weight to his words. I am such a believer in words, that I believe everything depends on who says them. Uncle Cornelius Heywood's story, told word for word by Uncle Timothy Warren, would not have been the same story at all. Not one of the listeners would have believed a syllable of it from the lips of round-bodied, red-faced, small-eyed, little Uncle Tim; whereas from Uncle Cornie,—disbelieve one of his stories if you could!

One word more concerning him. His interest in everything conjectured or believed relative to the awful borderland of this world and the next, was only equalled by his disgust at the vulgar, unimaginative forms which curiosity about such subjects has assumed in the present day. With a yearning after the unseen like that of a child for the lifting of the curtain of a theatre, he declared that, rather than accept such a spirit-world as the would-be seers of the nineteenth century thought or pretended to reveal,—the prophets of a pauperized, workhouse immortality, invented by a poverty-stricken soul, and a sense so greedy that it would gorge on carrion,—he would rejoice to believe that a man had just as much of a soul as the cabbage of Iamblichus, namely, an aerial double of his body.

"I'm so glad you're come, uncle!" said Kate. "Why

wouldn't you come to dinner? We have been so gloomy!"

"Well, Katey, you know I don't admire eating. I never could bear to see a cow tearing up the grass with her long tongue." As he spoke he looked very much like a cow. He had a way of opening his jaws while he kept his lips closely pressed together, that made his cheeks fall in, and his face look awfully long and dismal. "I consider eating," he went on, "such an animal exercise that it ought always to be performed in private. You never saw me dine, Kate."

"Never, uncle; but I have seen you drink;—nothing but water, I must confess."

"Yes, that is another affair. According to one eye-witness, that is no more than the disembodied can do. I must confess, however, that, although well attested, the story is to me scarcely credible. Fancy a glass of Bavarian beer lifted into the air without a visible hand, turned upside down, and set empty on the table!—and no splash on the floor or anywhere else!"

A solitary gleam of humour shone through the great eyes of the spectacles as he spoke.

"Oh, uncle! how can you believe such nonsense!" said Janet.

"I did not say I believed it,—did I? But why not? The story has at least a touch of imagination in it."

"That is a strange reason for believing a thing, uncle," said Harry.

"You might have a worse, Harry. I grant it is not sufficient; but it is better than that commonplace aspect which is the ground of most faith. I believe I did say that the story puzzled me."

"But how can you give it any quarter at all, uncle?"

"It does me no harm. There it is,—between the boards of an old German book. There let it remain."

103

"Well, you will never persuade me to believe such things," said Janet.

"Wait till I ask you, Janet," returned her uncle, gravely. "I have not the slightest desire to convince you. How did we get into this unprofitable current of talk? We will change it at once. How are consols, Harry?"

"Oh, uncle!" said Kate, "we were longing for a story, and just as I thought you were coming to one, off you go to consols!"

"I thought a ghost story at least was coming," said Janet.

"You did your best to stop it, Janet," said Harry.

Janet began an angry retort, but Cornelius interrupted her. "You never heard me tell a ghost story, Janet."

"You have just told one about a drinking ghost, uncle," said Janet,—in such a tone that Cornelius replied:

"Well, take that for your story, and let us talk of something else."

Janet apparently saw that she had been rude, and said as sweetly as she might,—"Ah! but you didn't make that one, uncle. You got it out of a German book."

"Make it!—Make a ghost story!" repeated Cornelius. "No; that I never did."

"Such things are not to be trifled with, are they?" said Janet.

"I at least have no inclination to trifle with them."

"But, really and truly, uncle," persisted Janet, "you don't believe in such things?"

"Why should I either believe or disbelieve in them? They are not essential to salvation, I presume."

"You must do the one or the other, I suppose."

"I beg your pardon. You suppose wrong. It would take twice the proof I have ever had to make me believe in them; and exactly your prejudice, and allow me to say ignorance, to make me disbelieve in them. Neither is within my reach. I postpone judgment. But you, young people, of course, are wiser, and know all about the question."

"Oh, uncle! I'm so sorry!" said Kate. "I am sure I did not mean to vex you."

"Not at all, not at all, my dear. —It wasn't you."

"Do you know," Kate went on, anxious to prevent anything unpleasant, for there was something very black perched on Janet's forehead, —"I have taken to reading about that kind of thing."

"I beg you will give it up at once. You will bewilder your brains till you are ready to believe anything, if only it be absurd enough. Nay, you may come to find the element of vulgarity essential to belief. I should be sorry to the heart to believe concerning a horse or dog what they tell you now-a-days about Shakespeare and Burns. What have you been reading, my girl?"

"Don't be alarmed, uncle. Only some Highland legends, which are too absurd either for my belief or for your theories."

"I don't know that, Kate."

"Why, what could you do with such shapeless creatures as haunt their fords and pools for instance? They are as featureless as the faces of the mountains."

"And so much the more terrible."

"But that does not make it easier to believe in them," said Harry.

"I only said," returned his uncle, "that their shapelessness adds to their horror."

"But you allowed, —almost, at least, uncle," said Kate, "that you could find a place in your theories even for those shapeless creatures."

Cornelius sat silent for a moment; then, having first doubled the length of his face, and restored it to its natural condition, said thoughtfully, —"I suspect,

Katey, if you were to come upon an ichthyosaurus or a pterodactyl asleep in the shrubbery, you would hardly expect your report of it to be believed all at once either by Harry or Janet."

"I suppose not, uncle. But I can't see what—— "

"Of course such a thing could not happen here and now. But there was a time when and a place where such a thing may have happened. Indeed, in my time, a traveller or two have got pretty soundly disbelieved for reporting what they saw,—the last of an expiring race, which had strayed over the natural verge of its history, coming to life in some neglected swamp, it-self a remnant of the slime of Chaos."

"I never heard you talk like that before, uncle," said Harry. "If you go on like that, you'll land me in a swamp, I'm afraid."

"I wasn't talking to you at all, Harry. Kate chal-lenged me to find a place for kelpies, and such like, in the theories she does me the honour of supposing I cultivate."

"Then you think, uncle, that all these stories are only legends which, if you could follow them up, would lead you back to some one of the awful mon-sters that have since quite disappeared from the earth."

"It is possible those stories may be such legends; but that was not what I intended to lead you to. I gave you that only as something like what I am going to say now. What if,—mind, I only suggest it,—what if the direful creatures, whose report lingers in these tales, should have an origin far older still? What if they were the remnants of a vanishing period of the earth's history long antecedent to the birth of mast-odon and iguanodon; a stage, namely, when the world, as we call it, had not yet become quite visible, was not yet so far finished as to part from the invisible world that was its mother, and which, on its part, had not then become quite invisible,—was only almost such; and when, as a credible consequence, strange shapes of those now invisible regions, Gorgons and Chimaeras dire, might be expected to gloom out occasionally from the awful Fauna of an ever-generating world upon that one which was being born of it. Hence, the life-periods of a world being long and slow, some of these huge, unformed bulks of half-created matter might, somehow, like the megatherium of later times,—a baby creation to them,—roll at age-long intervals, clothed in a mighty terror of shapelessness, into the half-recognition of human beings, whose consternation at the uncertain vision were barrier enough to prevent all further knowledge of its substance."

"I begin to have some notion of your meaning, uncle," said Kate.

"But then," said Janet, "all that must be over by this time. That world has been invisible now for many years."

"Ever since you were born, I suppose, Janet. The changes of a world are not to be measured by the changes of its generations."

"Oh, but, uncle, there can't be any such things. You know that as well as I do."

"Yes, just as well, and no better."

"There can't be any ghosts now. Nobody believes such things."

"Oh, as to ghosts, that is quite another thing. I did not know you were talking with reference to them. It is no wonder if one can get nothing sensible out of you, Janet, when your discrimination is no greater than to lump everything marvellous, kelpies, ghosts, vampires, doubles, witches, fairies, nightmares, and I don't know what all, under the one head of ghosts; and we hadn't been saying a word about them. If one were to disprove to you the existence of the afreets

107

of Eastern tales, you would consider the whole argument concerning the reappearance of the departed upset. I congratulate you on your powers of analysis and induction, Miss Janet. But it matters very little whether we believe in ghosts, as you say, or not, provided we believe that we are ghosts,—that within this body, which so many people are ready to consider their own very selves, there lies a ghostly embryo, at least, which has an inner side to it God only can see, which says *I* concerning itself, and which will soon have to know whether or not it can appear to those whom it has left behind, and thus solve the question of ghosts for itself, at least."

"Then you do believe in ghosts, uncle?" said Janet, in a tone that certainly was not respectful.

"Surely I said nothing of the sort, Janet. The man most convinced that he had himself had such an interview as you hint at, would find,—ought to find it impossible to convince any one else of it."

"You are quite out of my depth, uncle," said Harry. "Surely any honest man ought to be believed?"

"Honesty is not all, by any means, that is necessary to being believed. It is impossible to convey a conviction of anything. All you can do is to convey a conviction that you are convinced. Of course, what satisfied you might satisfy another; but, till you can present him with the sources of your conviction, you cannot present him with the conviction,—and perhaps not even then."

"You can tell him all about it, can't you?"

"Is telling a man about a ghost, affording him the source of your conviction? Is it the same as a ghost appearing to him? Really, Harry!—You cannot even convey the impression a dream has made upon you."

"But isn't that just because it is only a dream?"

"Not at all. The impression may be deeper and clearer on your mind than any fact of the next morning will make. You will forget the next day altogether, but the impression of the dream will remain through all the following whirl and storm of what you call facts. Now a conviction may be likened to a deep impression on the judgment or the reason, or both. No one can feel it but the person who is convinced. It cannot be conveyed."

"I fancy that is just what those who believe in spirit-rapping would say."

"There are the true and false of convictions, as of everything else. I mean that a man may take that for a conviction in his own mind which is not a conviction, but only resembles one. But those to whom you refer profess to appeal to facts. It is on the ground of those facts, and with the more earnestness the more reason they can give for receiving them as facts, that I refuse all their deductions with abhorrence. I mean that, if what they say is true, the thinker must reject with contempt the claim to anything like revelation therein."

"Then you do not believe in ghosts, after all?" said Kate, in a tone of surprise.

"I did not say so, my dear. Will you be reasonable, or will you not?"

"Dear uncle, do tell us what you really think."

"I have been telling you what I think ever since I came, Katey; and you won't take in a word I say."

"I have been taking in every word, uncle, and trying hard to understand it as well.—Did you ever see a ghost, uncle?"

Cornelius Heywood was silent. He shut his lips and opened his jaws till his cheeks almost met in the vacuum. A strange expression crossed the strange countenance, and the great eyes of his spectacles looked as if, at the very moment, they were seeing something no other spectacles could see. Then his jaws closed with a snap, his countenance brightened,

109

a flash of humour came through the goggle eyes of pebble, and, at length, he actually smiled as he said— "Really, Katey, you must take me for a simpleton!"

"How, uncle?"

"To think, if I had ever seen a ghost, I would confess the fact before a set of creatures like you,—all spinning your webs like so many spiders to catch and devour old Daddy Longlegs."

By this time Harry had grown quite grave. "Indeed, I am very sorry, uncle," he said, "if I have deserved such a rebuke."

"No, no, my boy," said Cornelius; "I did not mean it more than half. If I had meant it, I would not have said it. If you really would like——" Here he paused.

"Indeed we should, uncle." said Kate, earnestly. "You should have heard what we were saying just before you came in."

"All you were saying, Katey?"

"Yes," answered Kate, thoughtfully, "The worst we said was that you could not tell a story without—— well, we did say tacking a moral to it."

"Well, well! I musn't push it. A man has no right to know what people say about him. It unfits him for occupying his real position amongst them. He, least of all, has anything to do with it. If his friends won't defend him, he can't defend himself. Besides, what people say is so often untrue!—I don't mean to others, but to themselves. Their hearts are more honest than their mouths. But Janet doesn't want a strange story, I am sure."

Janet certainly was not one to have chosen for a listener to such a tale. Her eyes were so small that no satisfaction could possibly come of it. "Oh! I don't mind, uncle," she said, with half-affected indifference, as she searched in her box for silk to mend her gloves.

"You are not very encouraging, I must say," returned her uncle, making another cow-face.

"I will go away, if you like," said Janet, pretending to rise.

"No, never mind," said her uncle hastily. "If you don't want me to tell it, I want you to hear it; and, before I have done, that may have come to the same thing perhaps."

"Then you really are going to tell us a ghost-story!" said Kate, drawing her chair nearer to her uncle's; and then, finding this did not satisfy her sense of propinquity to the source of the expected pleasure, drawing a stool from the corner, and seating herself almost on the hearth-rug at his knee.

"I did not say so," returned Cornelius, once more. "I said I would tell you a strange story. You may call it a ghost-story if you like; I do not pretend to determine what it is. I confess it will look like one though."

After so many delays, Uncle Cornelius now plunged almost hurriedly into his narration.

"In the year 1820," he said, "in the month of August, I fell in love." Here the girls glanced at each other. The idea of Uncle Cornie in love, and in the very same century in which they were now listening to the confession, was too astonishing to pass without ocular remark; but, if he observed it, he took no notice of it; he did not even pause. "In the month of September, I was refused. Consequently, in the month of October, I was ready to fall in love again. Take particular care of yourself, Harry, for a whole month, at least, after your first disappointment; for you will never be more likely to do a foolish thing. Please yourself after the second. If you are silly then, you may take what you get, for you will deserve it,—except it be good fortune."

"Did you do a foolish thing then, uncle?" asked Harry, demurely.

"I did, as you will see; for I fell in love again."

"I don't see anything so very foolish in that."

"I have repented it since, though. Don't interrupt me again, please. In the middle of October, then, in the year 1820, in the evening, I was walking across Russell Square, on my way home from the British Museum, where I had been reading all day. You see I have a full intention of being precise, Janet."

"I'm sure I don't know why you make the remark to me, uncle," said Janet, with an involuntary toss of her head. Her uncle only went on with his narrative.

"I begin at the very beginning of my story," he said; "for I want to be particular as to everything that can appear to have had anything to do with what came afterwards. I had been reading, I say, all the morning in the British Museum; and, as I walked, I took off my spectacles to ease my eyes. I need not tell you that I am short-sighted now, for that you know well enough. But I must tell you that I was short-sighted then, and helpless enough without my spectacles, although I was not quite so much so as I am now;—for I find it all nonsense about short-sighted eyes improving with age. Well, I was walking along the south side of Russell Square, with my spectacles in my hand, and feeling a little bewildered in consequence,—for it was quite the dusk of the evening, and short-sighted people require more light than others. I was feeling, in fact, almost blind. I had got more than half-way to the other side, when, from the crossing that cuts off the corner in the direction of Montague Place, just as I was about to turn towards it, an old lady stepped upon the kerbstone of the pavement, looked at me for a moment, and passed,—an occurrence not very remarkable, certainly. But the lady was remarkable, and so was her dress. I am not good at observing, and I am still worse at describing dress; therefore, I can only say that hers reminded me of an old picture,—that is, I had never seen anything like it, except in old pictures. She had no bonnet, and looked as if she had walked straight out of an ancient drawing-room in her evening attire. Of her face I shall say nothing now. The next instant I met a man on the crossing, who stopped and addressed me. So short-sighted was I that, although I recognized his voice as one I ought to know, I could not identify him until I had put on my spectacles, which I did instinctively in the act of returning his greeting. At the same moment I glanced over my shoulder after the old lady. She was nowhere to be seen.

" 'What are you looking at?' asked James Hetheridge.

" 'I was looking after that old lady,' I answered, 'but I can't see her.'

" 'What old lady?' said Hetheridge, with just a touch of impatience.

" 'You must have seen her,' I returned. 'You were not more than three yards behind her.'

" 'Where is she then?'

" 'She must have gone down one of the areas, I think. But she looked a lady, though an old-fashioned one.'

" 'Have you been dining?' asked James in a tone of doubtful inquiry.

" 'No,' I replied, not suspecting the insinuation, 'I have only just come from the Museum.'

" 'Then I advise you to call on your medical man before you go home.'

" 'Medical man!' I returned; 'I have no medical man. What do you mean? I never was better in my life.'

" 'I mean that there was no old lady. It was an illusion, and that indicates something wrong. Besides, you did not know me when I spoke to you.'

" 'That is nothing,' I returned, 'I had just taken off

113

my spectacles, and without them I shouldn't know my own father.'

" 'How was it you saw the old lady, then?'

"The affair was growing serious under my friend's cross-questioning. I did not at all like the idea of his supposing me subject to hallucinations. So I answered, with a laugh, 'Ah! to be sure, that explains it. I am so blind without my spectacles, that I shouldn't know an old lady from a big dog.'

" 'There was no big dog,' said Hetheridge, shaking his head, as the fact for the first time dawned upon me that, although I had seen the old lady clearly enough to make a sketch of her, even to the features of her careworn, eager old face, I had not been able to recognise the well-known countenance of James Hetheridge.

" 'That's what comes of reading till the optic nerve is weakened,' he went on. 'You will cause yourself serious injury if you do not pull up in time. I'll tell you what; I'm going home next week,—will you go with me?'

" 'You are very kind,' I answered, not altogether rejecting the proposal, for I felt that a little change to the country would be pleasant, and I was quite my own master. For I had unfortunately means equal to my wants, and had no occasion to follow any profession,—not a very desirable thing for a young man, I can tell you, Master Harry. I need not keep you over the commonplaces of pressing and yielding. It is enough to say that he pressed and that I yielded. The day was fixed for our departure together; but something or other, I forget what, occurred, to make him advance the date, and it was resolved that I should follow later in the month.

"It was a drizzly afternoon in the beginning of the last week of October when I left the town of Bradford in a post-chaise to drive to Lewton Grange, the property of my friend's father. I had hardly left the town, and the twilight had only begun to deepen, when, glancing from one of the windows of the chaise, I fancied I saw, between me and the hedge, the dim figure of a horse keeping pace with us. I thought, in the first interval of unreason, that it was a shadow from my own horse, but reminded myself the next moment that there could be no shadow where there was no light. When I looked again, I was at the first glance convinced that my eyes had deceived me. At the second, I believed once more that a shadowy something, with the movements of a horse in harness, was keeping pace with us. I turned away again with some discomfort, and not till we had reached an open moorland road, whence a little watery light was visible on the horizon, could I summon up courage enough to look out once more. Certainly then there was nothing to be seen, and I persuaded myself that it had been all a fancy, and lighted a cigar. With my feet on the cushions before me, I had soon lifted myself on the clouds of tobacco far above all the terrors of the night, and believed them banished for ever. But, my cigar coming to an end just as we turned into the avenue that led up the Grange, I found myself once more glancing nervously out of the window. The moment the trees were about me, there was, if not a shadowy horse out there by the side of the chaise, yet certainly more than half that conviction in here in my consciousness. When I saw my friend, however, standing on the doorstep, dark against the glow of the hall-fire, I forgot all about it; and I need not add that I did not make it a subject of conversation when I entered, for I was well aware that it was essential to a man's reputation that his senses should be accurate, though his heart might without prejudice swarm with shadows, and his judgment be a very stable of hobbies.

"I was kindly received. Mrs. Hetheridge had been dead for some years, and Laetitia, the eldest of the family, was at the head of the household. She had two sisters, little more than girls. The father was a burly, yet gentlemanlike Yorkshire squire, who ate well, drank well, looked radiant, and hunted twice a week. In this pastime his son joined him when in the humour, which happened scarcely so often. I, who had never crossed a horse in my life, took his apology for not being able to mount me very coolly, assuring him that I would rather loiter about with a book than be in at the death of the best-hunted fox in Yorkshire.

"I very soon found myself at home with the Hetheridges; and very soon again I began to find myself not so much at home; for Miss Hetheridge,—Laetitia as I soon ventured to call her,—was fascinating. I have told you, Katey, that there was an empty place in my heart. Look to the door then, Katey. That was what made me so ready to fall in love with Laetitia. Her figure was graceful, and I think, even now, her face would have been beautiful but for a certain contraction of the skin over the nostrils, suggesting an invisible thumb and forefinger pinching them, which repelled me, although I did not then know what it indicated. I had not been with her one evening before the impression it made on me had vanished, and that so entirely that I could hardly recall the perception of the peculiarity which had occasioned it. Her observation was remarkably keen, and her judgment generally correct. She had great confidence in it herself; nor was she devoid of sympathy with some of the forms of human imagination, only they never seemed to possess for her any relation to practical life. That was to be ordered by the judgment alone. I do not mean she ever said so. I am only giving the conclusions I came to afterwards. It is not necessary that you should have any more thorough acquaintance with her mental character. One point in her moral nature, of especial consequence to my narrative, will show itself by and by.

"I did all I could to make myself agreeable to her, and the more I succeeded the more delightful she became in my eyes. We walked in the garden and grounds together; we read, or rather I read and she listened;—read poetry, Katey—sometimes till we could not read any more for certain hazinesses and huskinesses which look now, I am afraid, considerably more absurd than they really were, or even ought to look. In short, I considered myself thoroughly in love with her."

"And wasn't she in love with you uncle?"

"Don't interrupt me, child. I don't know. Honestly, I don't know. I hoped so then. I hope the contrary now. She liked me I am sure. That is not much to say. Liking is very pleasant and very cheap. Love is as rare as a star."

"I thought the stars were anything but rare, uncle."

"That's because you never went out to find one for yourself, Katey. They would prove a few miles apart then."

"But it would be big enough when I did find it."

"Right, my dear. That is the way with love.—Laetitia was a good housekeeper. Everything was punctual as clockwork. I use the word advisedly. If her father, who was punctual to one date,—the dinner-hour,—made any remark to the contrary as he took up the carving-knife, Laetitia would instantly send one of her sisters to question the old clock in the hall, and report the time to half a minute. It was sure to be found that, if there was a mistake, the mistake was in the clock. But although it was certainly a virtue to have her household in such perfect order, it was not a virtue to be impatient with every infringement of its rules on the part of others. She was very severe, for instance, upon her two younger sisters if, the moment after the second bell had rung, they were not seated at the dinner-table, washed and aproned. Order was a very idol with her. Hence the house was too tidy for any sense of comfort. If you left an open book on the table, you would, on returning to the room a moment after, find it put aside. What the furniture of the drawing-room was like, I never saw; for not even on Christmas Day, which was the last day I spent there, was it uncovered. Everything in it was kept in bibs and pinafores. Even the carpet was covered with a cold and slippery sheet of brown holland. Mr. Hetheridge never entered that room, and therein was wise. James remonstrated once. She answered him quite kindly, even playfully, but no change followed. What was worse, she made very wretched tea. Her father never took tea; neither did James. I was rather fond of it, but I soon gave it up. Everything her father partook of was first-rate. Everything else was somewhat poverty-stricken. My pleasure in Laetitia's society prevented me from making practical deductions from such trifles."

"I shouldn't have thought you knew anything about eating, uncle," said Janet.

"The less a man eats, the more he likes to have it good, Janet. In short,—there can be no harm in saying it now,—Laetitia was so far from being like the name of her baptism,—and most names are so good that they are worth thinking about; no children are named after bad ideas,—Laetitia was so far unlike hers as to be stingy,—an abominable fault. But, I repeat, the notion of such a fact was far from me then. And now for my story.

"The first of November was a very lovely day, quite one of the 'halcyon days' of 'St. Martin's summer.' I was sitting in a little arbour I had just discovered, with a book in my hand,—not reading, however, but day-dreaming,—when, lifting my eyes from the ground, I was startled to see, through a thin shrub in front of the arbour, what seemed the form of an old lady seated, apparently reading from a book on her knee. The sight instantly recalled the old lady of Russell Square. I started to my feet, and then, clear of the intervening bush, saw only a great stone such as abounded on the moors in the neighbourhood, with a lump of quartz set on the top of it. Some childish taste had put it there for an ornament. Smiling at my own folly, I sat down again, and reopened my book. After reading for a while, I glanced up again, and once more started to my feet, overcome by the fancy that there verily sat the old lady reading. You will say it indicated an excited condition of the brain. Possibly; but I was, as far as I can recall, quite collected and reasonable. I was almost vexed this second time, and sat down once more to my book. Still, every time I looked up, I was startled afresh. I doubt, however, if the trifle is worth mentioning, or has any significance even in relation to what followed.

"After dinner I strolled out by myself, leaving father and son over their claret. I did not drink wine; and from the lawn I could see the windows of the library, whither Laetitia commonly retired from the dinner-table. It was a very lovely soft night. There was no moon, but the stars looked wider awake than usual. Dew was falling, but the grass was not yet wet, and I wandered about on it for half an hour. The stillness was somehow strange. It had a wonderful feeling in it as if something were expected,—as if the quietness were the mould in which some event or other was about to be cast.

"Even then I was a reader of certain sorts of recondite lore. Suddenly I remembered that this was the eve of All Souls. This was the night on which the dead came out of their graves to visit their old homes.

'Poor dead!' I thought with myself; 'have you any place to call a home now? If you have, surely you will not wander back here, where all that you called home has either vanished or given itself to others, to be their home now and yours no more! What an awful doom the old fancy has allotted you! To dwell in your graves all the year, and creep out, this one night, to enter at the midnight door, left open for welcome! A poor welcome truly!—just an open door, a clean-swept floor, and a fire to warm your rain-sodden limbs! The household asleep, and the house-place swarming with the ghosts of ancient times,—the miser, the spend-thrift, the profligate, the coquette,—for the good ghosts sleep, and are troubled with no waking like yours! Not one man, sleepless like yourselves, to question you, and be answered after the fashion of the old nursery rhyme: —

" 'What makes your eyes so holed?'
'I've laid so long among the mould.'
'What makes your feet so broad?'
'I've walked more than ever I rode!' "

" 'Yet who can tell?' I went on to myself. 'It may be your hell to return thus. It may be that only on this one night of all the year you can show yourselves to him who can see you, but that the place where you were wicked is the Hades to which you are doomed for ages.' I thought and thought till I began to feel the air alive about me, and was enveloped in the vapours that dim the eyes of those who strain them for one peep through the dull mica windows that will not open on the world of ghosts. At length I cast my fancies away, and fled from them to the library, where the bodily presence of Laetitia made the world of ghosts appear shadowy indeed.

"What a reality there is about a bodily presence!'

I said to myself, as I took my chamber-candle in my hand. 'But what is there more real in a body?' I said again, as I crossed the hall. 'Surely nothing,' I went on, as I ascended the broad staircase to my room. 'The body must vanish. If there be a spirit, that will remain. A body can but vanish. A ghost can appear.'

"I woke in the morning with a sense of such discomfort as made me spring out of bed at once. My foot lighted upon my spectacles. How they came to be on the floor I could not tell, for I never took them off when I went to bed. When I lifted them I found they were in two pieces; the bridge was broken. This was awkward. I was so utterly helpless without them! Indeed, before I could lay my hand on my hair-brush I had to peer through one eye of the parted pair. When I looked at my watch after I was dressed, I found I had risen an hour earlier than usual. I groped my way down-stairs to spend the hour before breakfast in the library.

"No sooner was I seated with a book than I heard the voice of Laetitia scolding the butler, in no very gentle tones, for leaving the garden-door open all night. The moment I heard this, the strange occurrences I am about to relate began to dawn upon my memory. The door had been open the night long between All Saints and All Souls. In the middle of that night I awoke suddenly. I knew it was not the morning by the sensations I had, for the night feels altogether different from the morning. It was quite dark. My heart was beating violently, and I either hardly could or hardly dared breathe. A nameless terror was upon me, and my sense of hearing was, apparently by the force of its expectation, unnaturally roused and keen. There it was,—a slight noise in the room!— slight, but clear, and with an unknown significance about it! It was awful to think it would come again. I do believe it was only one of those creaks in the timbers which announce the torpid, age-long, sinking flow of every house back to the dust,—a motion to which the flow of the glacier is as a torrent, but which is no less inevitable and sure. Day and night it ceases not; but only in the night, when house and heart are still, do we hear it. No wonder it should sound fearful! for are we not the immortal dwellers in ever-crumbling clay? The clay is so near us, and yet not of us, that its every movement starts a fresh dismay. For what will its final ruin disclose? When it falls from about us, where shall we find that we have existed all the time?

"My skin tingled with the bursting of the moisture from its pores. Something was in the room beside me. A confused, indescribable sense of utter loneliness, and yet awful presence, was upon me, mingled with a dreary, hopeless desolation, as of burnt-out love and aimless life. All at once I found myself sitting up. The terror that a cold hand might be laid upon me, or a cold breath blow on me, or a corpse-like face bend down through the darkness over me, had broken my bonds!—I would meet half way whatever might be approaching. The moment that my will burst into action the terror began to ebb.

"The room in which I slept was a large one, perfectly dreary with tidiness. I did not know till afterwards that it was Laetitia's room, which she had given up to me rather than prepare another. The furniture, all but one article, was modern and commonplace. I could not help remarking to myself afterwards how utterly void the room was of the nameless charm of feminine occupancy. I had seen nothing to wake a suspicion of its being a lady's room. The article I have excepted was an ancient bureau, elaborate and ornate, which stood on one side of the large bow window. The very morning before, I had seen a bunch of keys hanging from the upper part of it, and had peeped in. Finding, however, that the pigeon-holes were full of papers, I closed it at once. I should have been glad to use it, but clearly it was not for me. At that bureau the figure of a woman was now seated in the posture of one writing. A strange, dim light was around her, but whence it proceeded I never thought of inquiring. As if I, too, had stepped over the bourne, and was a ghost myself, all fear was now gone. I got out of bed, and softly crossed the room to where she

was seated. 'If she should be beautiful!' I thought,—
for I had often dreamed of a beautiful ghost that made
love to me. The figure did not move. She was looking
at a faded brown paper. 'Some old love-letter,' I
thought, and stepped nearer. So cool was I now, that
I actually peeped over her shoulder. With mingled
surprise and dismay I found that the dim page over
which she bent was that of an old account-book. Ancient household records, in rusty ink, held up to the
glimpses of the waning moon, which shone through
the parting in the curtains, their entries of shillings
and pence!—Of pounds there was not one. No doubt
pounds and farthings are much the same in the world
of thought—the true spirit-world; but in the ghost-
world this eagerness over shillings and pence must
mean something awful! To think that coins which
had since been worn smooth in other pockets and
purses, which had gone back to the mint, and been
melted down, to come out again and yet again with
the heads of new kings and queens,—that dinners,
eaten by men and women and children whose bodies
had since been eaten by the worms,—that polish for
the floors, inches of whose thickness had since been
worn away,—that the hundred nameless trifles of a
life utterly vanished, should be perplexing, annoying,
and worst of all, interesting the soul of a ghost who
had been in Hades for centuries! The writing was
very old-fashioned, and the words were contracted.
I could read nothing but the moneys and one single
entry,—'Corinths, Vs.'

"Currants for a Christmas pudding, most likely!—
Ah, poor lady! the pudding and not the Christmas
was her care; not the delight of the children over it,
but the beggarly pence which it cost. And she cannot
get it out of her head, although her brain was 'pow-
dered all as thin as flour' ages ago in the mortar of
Death. 'Alas, poor ghost!' It needs no treasured hoard

left behind, no floor stained with the blood of the murdered child, no wickedly hidden parchment of landed rights!—An old account-book is enough for the hell of the house-keeping gentle-woman!

"She never lifted her face, or seemed to know that I stood behind her. I left her, and went into the bow window, where I could see her face. I was right. It was the same old lady I had met in Russell Square, walking in front of James Hetheridge. Her withered lips went moving as if they would have uttered words had the breath been commissioned thither; her brow was contracted over her thin nose; and once and again her shining forefinger went up to her temple as if she were pondering some deep problem of humanity. How long I stood gazing at her I do not know, but at last I withdrew to my bed, and left her struggling to solve that which she could never solve thus. It was the symbolic problem of her own life, and she had failed to read it. I remember nothing more. She may be sitting there still, solving at the insolvable.

"I should have felt no inclination, with the broad sun of the squire's face, the keen eyes of James, and the beauty of Laetitia before me at the breakfast-table, to say a word about what I had seen, even if I had not been afraid of the doubt concerning my sanity which the story would certainly awaken. What with the memories of the night and the want of my spectacles, I passed a very dreary day, dreading the return of the night, for, cool as I had been in her presence, I could not regard the possible reappearance of the ghost with equanimity. But when the night did come, I slept soundly till the morning.

"The next day, not being able to read with comfort, I went wandering about the place, and at length began to fit the outside and inside of the house together. It was a large and rambling edifice, parts of it very old, parts comparatively modern. I first found my own window, which looked out of the back. Below this window, on one side, there was a door. I wondered whither it led, but found it locked. At the moment James approached from the stables. 'Where does this door lead?' I asked him. 'I will get the key,' he answered. 'It is rather a queer old place. We used to like it when we were children.' 'There's a stair, you see,' he said, as he threw the door open. 'It leads up over the kitchen.' I followed him up the stair. 'There's a door into your room,' he said, 'but it's always locked now.—And here's Grannie's room, as they call it, though why, I have not the least idea,' he added, as he pushed open the door of an old-fashioned parlour, smelling very musty. A few old books lay on a side-table. A china bowl stood beside them, with some shrivelled, scentless rose-leaves in the bottom of it. The cloth that covered the table was riddled by moths, and the spider-legged chairs were covered with dust.

"A conviction seized me that the old bureau must have belonged to this room, and I soon found the place where I judged it must have stood. But the same moment I caught sight of a portrait on the wall above the spot I had fixed upon. 'By Jove!' I cried, involuntarily, 'that's the very old lady I met in Russell Square!"

" 'Nonsense!' said James. 'Old-fashioned ladies are like babies,—they all look the same. That's a very old portrait.'

" 'So I see,' I answered. 'It is like a Zucchero.'

" 'I don't know whose it is,' he answered hurriedly, and I thought he looked a little queer.

" 'Is she one of the family?' I asked.

" 'They say so; but who or what she was, I don't know. You must ask Letty,' he answered.

" 'The more I look at it,' I said, 'the more I am convinced it is the same old lady.'

" 'Well,' he returned with a laugh, 'my old nurse

used to say she was rather restless. But it's all nonsense.'

" 'That bureau in my room looks about the same date as this furniture,' I remarked.

" 'It used to stand just there,' he answered, pointing to the space under the picture. 'Well I remember with what awe we used to regard it; for they said the old lady kept her accounts at it still. We never dared touch the bundles of yellow papers in the pigeon-holes. I remember thinking Letty a very heroine once when she touched one of them with the tip of her forefinger. She had got yet more courageous by the time she had it moved into her own room.'

" 'Then that is your sister's room I am occupying?' I said.

" 'Yes.'

" 'I am ashamed of keeping her out of it.'

" 'Oh! she'll do well enough.'

" 'If I were she though,' I added, 'I would send that bureau back to its own place.'

" 'What do you mean, Heywood! Do you believe every old wife's tale that ever was told?'

" 'She may get a fright some day,—that's all!' I replied.

"He smiled with such an evident mixture of pity and contempt that for the moment I almost disliked him; and feeling certain that Laetitia would receive any such hint in a somewhat similar manner, I did not feel inclined to offer her any advice with regard to the bureau.

"Little occurred during the rest of my visit worthy of remark. Somehow or other I did not make much progress with Laetitia. I believe I had begun to see into her character a little, and therefore did not get deeper in love as the days went on. I know I became less absorbed in her society, although I was still anxious to make myself agreeable to her,—or perhaps, more properly, to give her a favourable impression of me. I do not know whether she perceived any difference in my behaviour, but I remember that I began again to remark the pinched look of her nose, and to be a little annoyed with her for always putting aside my book. At the same time, I daresay I was provoking, for I never was given to tidiness myself.

"At length Christmas Day arrived. After breakfast, the squire, James, and the two girls arranged to walk to church. Laetitia was not in the room at the moment. I excused myself on the ground of a headache, for I had had a bad night. When they left, I went up to my room, threw myself on the bed, and was soon fast asleep.

"How long I slept I do not know, but I woke again with that indescribable yet well-known sense of not being alone. The feeling was scarcely less terrible in the daylight than it had been in the darkness. With the same sudden effort as before, I sat up in the bed. There was the figure at the open bureau, in precisely the same position as on the former occasion. But I could not see it so distinctly. I rose as gently as I could, and approached it, after the first physical terror. I am not a coward. Just as I got near enough to see the account book open on the folding cover of the bureau, she started up, and, turning, revealed the face of Laetitia. She blushed crimson.

" 'I beg your pardon, Mr. Heywood,' she said, in great confusion; 'I thought you had gone to church with the rest.'

" 'I had lain down with a headache, and gone to sleep,' I replied. 'But,—forgive me, Miss Hetheridge,' I added, for my mind was full of the dreadful coincidence,—'don't you think you would have been better at church than balancing your accounts on Christmas Day?'

" 'The better day the better deed,' she said, with a somewhat offended air, and turned to walk from the room.

" 'Excuse me, Laetitia,' I resumed, very seriously, 'but I want to tell you something.'

"She looked conscious. It never crossed me, that perhaps she fancied I was going to make a confession. Far other things were then in my mind. For I thought how awful it was, if she too, like the ancestral ghost, should have to do an age-long penance of haunting the bureau and those horrid figures, and I had suddenly resolved to tell her the whole story. She listened with varying complexion and face half turned aside. When I had ended, which I fear I did with something of a personal appeal, she lifted her head and looked me in the face, with just a slight curl on her thin lip, and answered me. 'If I had wanted a sermon, Mr. Heywood, I should have gone to church for it. As for the ghost, I am sorry for you.' So saying she walked out of the room.

"The rest of the day I did not find very merry. I pleaded my headache as an excuse for going to bed early. How I hated the room now! Next morning, immediately after breakfast, I took my leave of Lewton Grange."

"And lost a good wife, perhaps, for the sake of a ghost, uncle!" said Janet.

"If I lost a wife at all, it was a stingy one. I should have been ashamed of her all my life long."

"Better than a spendthrift," said Janet.

"How do you know that?" returned her uncle. "All the difference I see is, that the extravagant ruins the rich, and the stingy robs the poor."

"But perhaps she repented, uncle," said Kate.

"I don't think she did, Katey. Look here."

Uncle Cornelius drew from the breast-pocket of his coat a black-edged letter.

"I have kept up my friendship with her brother," he said. "All he knows about the matter is, that either we had a quarrel, or she refused me;—he is not sure which. I must say for Laetitia, that she was no tattler. Well, here's a letter I had from James this very morning. I will read it to you.

" 'My dear Heywood,—We have had a terrible shock this morning. Letty did not come down to breakfast, and Lizzie went to see if she was ill. We heard her scream, and, rushing up, there was poor Letty, sitting at the old bureau, quite dead. She had fallen forward on the desk, and her housekeeping-book was crumpled up under her. She had been so all night long, we suppose, for she was not undressed, and was quite cold. The doctors say it was disease of the heart.'

"There!" said Uncle Cornie, folding up the letter.

"Do you think the ghost had anything to do with it, uncle?" asked Kate, almost under her breath.

"How should I know, my dear? Possibly."

"It's very sad," said Janet; "but I don't see the good of it all. If the ghost had come to tell that she had hidden away money in some secret place in the old bureau, one would see why she had been permitted to come back. But what was the good of those accounts after they were over and done with? I don't believe in the ghost."

"Ah, Janet, Janet! but those wretched accounts were not over and done with, you see. That is the misery of it."

Uncle Cornelius rose without another word, bade them good-night, and walked out into the wind.

THE BUTCHER'S BILLS

I: HUSBAND AND WIFE

I am going to tell a story of married life. My title will prepare the reader for something hardly heroic; but I trust it will not be found lacking in the one genuine and worthy interest a tale ought to have—namely, that it presents a door through which we may walk into one region or another of the human heart, and there find ourselves not altogether unacquainted or from home.

There was a law among the Jews which forbade the yoking together of certain animals, either because, being unequal in size or strength, one of them must be oppressed, or for the sake of some lesson thus embodied to the Eastern mind—possibly for both reasons. Half the tragedy would be taken out of social life if this law could be applied to human beings in their various relations. I do not say that this would be well, or that we could afford to lose the result of the tragedy thus occasioned. Neither do I believe that there are so many instances of unequal yoking as the misprising judgments of men by men and women by women might lead us to imagine. Not every one declared by the wisdom of acquaintance to have thrown himself or herself away must therefore be set down as unequally yoked. Or it may even be that the inequality is there, but the loss on the other side. How

Reprinted from *The Gifts of the Child Christ, and Other Tales* (1882).

some people could ever have come together must always be a puzzle until one knows the history of the affair; but not a few whom most of us would judge quite unsuited to each other do yet get on pretty well from the first, and better and better the longer they are together, and that with mutual advantage, improvement, and development. Essential humanity is deeper than the accidents of individuality; the common is more powerful than the peculiar; and the honest heart will always be learning to act more and more in accordance with the laws of its being. It must be of much more consequence to any lady that her husband should be a man on whose word she can depend than that he should be of a gracious presence. But if instead of coming nearer to a true understanding of each other, the two should from the first keep falling asunder, then something tragic may almost be looked for.

Duncan and Lucy Dempster were a couple the very mention of whose Christian names together would have seemed amusing to the friends who had long ceased to talk of their unfitness. Indeed, I doubt if in their innermost privacy they ever addressed each other except as Mr. and Mrs. Dempster. For the first time to see them together, no one could help wondering how the conjunction could have been effected. Dempster was of Scotch descent, but the hereditary high cheek-bone seemed to have got into his nose, which was too heavy a pendant for the low forehead from which it hung. About an inch from the end it took a swift and unexpected curve downwards, and was a curious and abnormal nose, which could not properly be assorted with any known class of noses. A long upper lip, a large, firm, and not quite ugly mouth, with a chin both long and square, completed a face which, with its low forehead, being yet longer than usual, had a particularly equine look. He was rather under the middle height, slender, and well enough made—altogether an ordinary mortal, known on 'Change as an able, keen, and laborious man of business. What his special business was I do not know. He went to the city by the eight o'clock omnibus every morning, dived into a court, entered a little square, rushed up two flights of stairs to a couple of rooms, and sat down in the back one before an office table on a hair-seated chair. It was a dingy place—not so dirty as it looked, I daresay. Even the windows, being of bad glass, did, I believe, look dirtier than they were. It was a place where, so far as the eye of an outsider could tell, much or nothing might be doing. Its occupant always wore his hat in it, and his hat always looked shabby. Some people said he was rich, others that he would be one day. Some said he was a responsible man, whatever the epithet may have been intended to mean. I believe he was quite as honest as the recognized laws of his trade demanded—and for how many could I say more? Nobody said he was avaricious—but then he moved amongst men whose very notion was first to make money, after that to be religious, or to enjoy themselves, as the case might be. And no one either ever said of him that he was a good man, or a generous. He was about forty years of age, looking somehow as if he had never been younger. He had had a fair education—better than is generally considered necessary for mercantile purposes—but it would have been hard to discover any signs of it in the spending of his leisure. On Sunday mornings he went with his wife to church, and when he came home had a good dinner, of which now and then a friend took his share. If no stranger was present he took his wine by himself, and went to sleep in his easy chair of maroon-coloured leather, while his wife sat on the other side of the fire if it was winter, or a little way off by the open window if it was summer, gently yawned now and then, and looked at him with eyes a little troubled. Then he went off again by the eight o'clock omnibus on Monday morning, and not an idea more or less had he in his head, not a hair's-breadth of difference was there in his conduct or pursuits, that he had been to church and had spent the day out of business. That may, however, for anything I know, have been as much the clergyman's fault as his. He was the sort of man you might call machine-made, one in whom humanity, if in no wise caricatured, was yet in no wise ennobled.

His wife was ten years younger than he—hardly less than beautiful—only that over her countenance seemed to have gathered a kind of haze of commonness. At first sight, notwithstanding, one could not help perceiving that she was china and he was delft. She was graceful as she sat, long-necked, slope-shouldered, and quite as tall as her husband, with a marked daintiness about her in the absence of the extremes of the fashion, in the quality of the lace she wore on her black silk dress, and in the wide white sleeves of fine cambric that covered her arms from the shoulder to the wrist. She had a morally delicate air, a look of scrupulous nicety and lavender-stored linen. She had long dark lashes; and when they rose, the eyelids revealed eyes of uncommon beauty. She had good features, good teeth, and a good complexion. The main feeling she produced and left was of ladyhood—little more.

Sunday afternoon came fifty-two times in the year. I mention this because then always, and nearly then only, could one calculate on seeing them together. It came to them in a suburb of London, and the look of it was dull. Doubtless Mr. Dempster's dinner and his repose after it were interesting to him, but I cannot help thinking his wife found it dreary. She had, however, got used to it. The house was a good old one, of red brick, much larger than they required, but not expensive, and had a general look of the refinement of its mistress. In the summer the windows of the dining-room would generally be open, for they looked into a really lovely garden behind the house, and the scent of the jasmine that crept all around them would come in plentifully. I wonder what the scent of jasmine did in Duncan Dempster's world. Perhaps it never got farther than the general antechamber of the sensorium. It often made his wife sad—she could not tell why. To him I daresay it smelt agreeable, but I can hardly believe it ever woke in him that dreamy sensation it gave her—of something she had not had enough of, she could not say what. When the heat was gone off a little he would walk out on the lawn, which was well kept and well watered, with many flowering shrubs about it. Why he did so, I cannot tell. He looked at nothing in particular, only walked about for a few minutes, no doubt derived some pleasure of a mild nature from something, and walked in again to tea. One might have expected he would have cultivated the acquaintance of his garden a little, if it were only for the pleasure the contrast would give him when he got back to his loved office, for a greater contrast could not well have been found than between his dingy dreary haunt on weekdays— a place which nothing but duty could have made other than repugnant to any free soul—and this nest of greenery and light and odour. Sweet scents floated in clouds invisible about the place; flower eyes and stars and bells and bunches shone and glowed and lurked all around; his very feet might have learned a lesson of that which is beyond the sense from the turf he trod; but all the time, if he were not exactly seeing in his mind's eye the walls and tables of his office in the City square, his thoughts were not the

less brooding over such business as he there trans-
acted. For Mr. Dempster's was not a free soul. How
could it be when all his energies were given to making
money? This he counted his *calling*—and I believe
actually contrived to associate some feeling of duty
with the notion of leaving behind him a plump round
sum of money, as if money in accumulation and following flood, instead of money in peaceful current,
were the good thing for the world! Hence the whole
realm of real life, the universe of thought and growth,
was a high-hedged park to him, within which he never
even tried to look—not even knowing that he was
shut out from it, for the hedge was of his own growing. What shall ever wake such a man to a sense of
indwelling poverty, or make him begin to hunger after
any lowliest expansion? Does a reader retort, "The
man was comfortable, and why should he be troubled?" If the end of being, I answer, is only comfort
in self, I yield. But what if there should be at the
heart of the universe a Thought to which the being
of such men is distasteful? What if to that Thought
they look blots in light, ugly things? May there not
lie in that direction some possible reason why they
should bethink themselves? Dempster, however, was
not yet a clinker out of which all the life was burned,
however much he looked like one. There was in him
that which might yet burn—and give light and heat.

On the Sunday evenings Mrs. Dempster would
have gladly gone to church again, if only—though to
herself she never allowed this for one of her reasons—to slip from under the weight of her husband's
presence. He seldom spoke to her more than a sentence at a time, but he did like to have her near him,
and I suppose held, through the bare presence, some
kind of dull one-sided communication with her; what
did a woman know about business? and what did he
know about except business? It is true he had a ru-

dimentary pleasure in music—and would sometimes ask her to play to him, when he would listen, and after his fashion enjoy. But although here was a gift that might be developed until his soul could echo the music of the spheres, the embodied souls of Handel or Mendelssohn were to him but clouds of sound wrapped about kernels—let me say of stock or bonds.

For a year or so after their marriage it had been the custom that, the first thing after breakfast on Monday morning, she should bring him her account-book, that they might together go over her week's expenses. She must cultivate the business habits in which, he said, he found her more than deficient. How could he endure in a wife what would have been preposterous in a clerk, and would have led to his immediate dismissal? It was in his eyes necessary that the same strict record of receipt and expenditure should be kept in the household as in the office; how else was one to know in what direction things were going? he said. He required of his wife, therefore, that every individual thing that cost money, even to what she spent upon her own person, should be entered in her book. She had no money of her own, neither did he allow her any special sum for her private needs; but he made her a tolerably liberal weekly allowance, from which she had to pay everything except house-rent and taxes, an arrangement which I cannot believe a good one, as it will inevitably lead some conscientious wives to self-denial severer than necessary, and on the other hand will tempt the vulgar nature to make a purse for herself by mean savings off everybody else. It was especially distasteful to Mrs. Dempster to have to set down every little article of personal requirement that she bought. It would probably have seemed to her but a trifle had they both been young when they married, and had there been that tenderness of love between them which so soon sets everything more than right; but as it was, she could never get over the feeling that the man was strange to her. As it was she would have got over this. But there was in her a certain constitutional lack of precision, combined with a want of energy and a weakness of will, that rendered her more than careless where her liking was not interested. Hence, while she would have been horrified at playing a wrong note or singing out of tune, she not only had no anxiety, for the thing's own sake, to have her accounts correct, but shrunk from every effort in that direction. Now I can perfectly understand her recoil from the whole affair, with her added dislike to the smallness of the thing required of her; but seeing she did begin with doing it after a fashion, it is not so easy to understand why, doing it, she should not make a consolation of doing it with absolute exactness. Not even her dread of her husband's dissatisfaction—which was by no means small—could prevail to make her, instead of still trusting a memory that constantly played her false, put down a thing at once, nor postpone it to a far less convenient season. Hence it came that her accounts, though never much out, never balanced; and the weekly audit, while it grew more and more irksome to the one, grew more and more unsatisfactory to the other. For to Mr. Dempster's dusty eyes exactitude wore the robe of rectitude, and before long, precisely and merely from the continued unsatisfactory condition of her accounts, he began, in a hidden corner of his righteous soul, to reflect on the moral condition of his wife herself as unsatisfactory. Now such it certainly was, but he was not the man to judge it correctly, or to perceive the true significance of her failing. In business, while scrupulous as to the requirements of custom and recognized right, he nevertheless did things from which her soul would have recoiled like "the tender horns of cockled snails";

yet it was to him not merely a strange and inexplicable fact that she should *never* be able to show a penny, nay, often not to a shilling or eighteenpence, how the week's allowance went, but a painful one as indicating something beyond perversity. And truly it was no very hard task he required of her, for, seeing they had no children, only three servants, and saw little company, her housekeeping could not be a very heavy or involved affair. Perhaps if it had been more difficult she would have done it better, but anyhow she hated the whole thing, procrastinated, and setting down several things together, was *sure* to forget some article or mistake some price; yet not one atom more would she distrust her memory the next time she was tempted. But it was a small fault at worst, and if her husband had loved her enough to understand the bearings of it in relation to her mental and moral condition he would have tried to content himself that at least she did not exceed her allowance; and would of all things have avoided making such a matter a burden upon the consciousness of one so differently educated, if not constituted, from himself. It is but fair to add on the other side that, if she had loved him after anything like a wifely ideal, which I confess was not yet possible to her, it would not have been many weeks before she had a first correct account to show him. Convinced, at length, that accuracy was not to be had from her, and satisfying himself with dissatisfaction, he one morning threw from him the little ruled book, and declared, in a wrath which he sought to smother into dignified but hopeless rebuke, that he would trouble himself with her no further. She burst into tears, took up the book, left the room, cried a little, resolved to astonish him the next Monday, and never set down another item. When it came, and breakfast was over, he gave her

the usual cheque, and left at once for town. Nor had
the accounts ever again been alluded to between them.

Now this might have been very well, or at least not
very ill, if both had done tolerably well thereafter—
that is, if the one had continued to attend to her expenditure as well as before, and the other, when he
threw away the account-book, had dismissed from
his mind the whole matter. But Dempster was one
of those dangerous men—more dangerous, however,
to themselves than to others—who never forget, that
is, get over, an offence or disappointment. They respect themselves so much, and, out of their respect
for themselves, build so much upon success, set so
much by never being defeated but always gaining their
point, that when they are driven to confess themselves foiled, the confession is made from the "poor
dumb mouth" of a wound that cannot be healed. It
is there for ever—will be there at least until they find
another God to worship than their own paltry selves.
Hence it came that the bourn between the two spiritual estates yawned a little wider at one point, and
a mist of dissatisfaction would not infrequently rise
from a certain stagnant pool in its hollow. The cause
was paltry in one sense, but nothing to which belongs the name of *Cause* can fail to mingle the element
of awfulness even with its paltriness. Its worst effect
was that it hindered approximation in other parts of
their matching natures.

And so to Mrs. Dempster, I am sorry for the apparent justification which what I have to confess concerning her must give to the severe whims of such
husbands as hers: from that very Monday morning
she began to grow a little careless about her expenditure—which she had never been before. By degrees
bill after bill was allowed to filch from the provision
of the following week, and when that was devoured,
then from that of the week after. It was not that she

was in the least more expensive upon herself, or that she consciously wasted anything; but, altogether averse to housekeeping, she ceased to exercise the same outlook upon the expenditure of the house, did not keep her horses together, left the management more and more to her cook; while the consciousness that she was not doing her duty made her more and more uncomfortable, and the knowledge that things were going farther and farther wrong, made her hate the idea of accounts worse and worse, until she came at length to regard them with such a loathing as might have fitted some extreme of moral evil. The bills which were supposed by her husband to be regularly settled every week were at last months behind, and the week's money spent in meeting the most pressing of its demands, while what it could no longer cover was cast upon the growing heap of evil for the time to come.

I must say this for her, however, that there was a small sum of money she expected on the death of a crazy aunt, which, if she could but lay hold of it without her husband's knowledge, she meant to devote to the clearing off of everything, when she vowed to herself to do better in the time to come.

The worst thing in it all was that her fear of her husband kept increasing, and that she felt more and more uncomfortable in his presence. Hence that troubled look in her eye, always more marked when her husband sat dozing in his chair of a Sunday afternoon.

It was natural, too, that, although they never quarrelled, their intercourse should not grow of a more tender character. Seldom was there a salient point in their few scattered sentences of conversation, except, indeed, it were some piece of news either had to communicate. Occasionally the wife read something from the newspaper, but never except at her husband's request. In general he enjoyed his newspaper over a chop at his office. Two or three times since their marriage—now eight years—he had made a transient resolve pointing at the improvement of her mind, and to that end had taken from his great glass-armoured bookcase some *standard* work—invariably, I believe, upon party-politics—from which he had made her read him a chapter. But, unhappily, she had always got to the end of it without gaining the slightest glimmer of a true notion of what the author was driving at.

It almost moves me to pity to think of the vagueness of that rudimentary humanity in Mr. Dempster which made him dream of doing something to improve his wife's mind. What did he ever do to improve his own? It is hard to understand how horses find themselves so comfortable in their stables that, be the day ever so fine, the country ever so lovely, the air ever so exhilarating, they are always rejoiced to get back into their dull twilight: it is harder for me to understand how Mr. Dempster could be so comfortable in his own mind that he never wanted to get out of it, even at the risk of being beside himself; but no doubt the dimness of its twilight had a good deal to do with his content. And then there is that in every human mind which no man's neighbour, nay, no man himself, can understand. My neighbour may in his turn be regarding my mind as a gloomy place to live in, while I find it no undesirable residence—though chiefly because of the number of windows it affords me for looking out of it. Still, if Dempster's dingy office in the City was not altogether a sufficing type of the mind that used it, I consider it a very fairly good one.

But wherein was Mrs. Dempster so very different from her husband as I rudely fancy some of my readers imagining her? Whatever may have been her reasons for marrying him—one would suppose they must have been weighty—to do so she must have been in a very undeveloped condition, and in that condition she still remained. I do not mean that she was less developed than ninety-nine out of the hundred: most women affect me only as valuable crude material out of which precious things are making. How much they might be, must be, shall be! For now they stand like so many Lot's-wives—so many rough-hewn marble blocks, rather, of which a Divinity is shaping the ends. Mrs. Dempster had all the making of a lovely woman, but notwithstanding her grace, her beauty, her sweetness, her lark-like ballading too, she was a very ordinary woman in that region of her which knew what she meant when she said "I." Of this fact she had hardly a suspicion, however; for until aspiration brings humility, people are generally pretty well satisfied with themselves, having no idea what poor creatures they are. She saw in her mirror a superior woman, regarded herself as one of the finer works of creation. The worst was that from the first she had counted herself superior to her husband, and in marrying him had felt not merely that she was conferring a favour, which every husband would allow, but that she was lowering herself without elevating him. Now it is true that she was pleasanter to look at, that her manners were sweeter, and her notions of the becoming far less easily satisfied than his; also that she was a little less deficient in vague reverence for certain forms of the higher than he. But I know of nothing in her to determine her classification as of greater value than he, except indeed that she was on the whole rather more honest. She read novels and he did not; she passed shallow judgment, where he scorned to judge; she read all the middling poetry that came in her way, and copied books full of it; but she could no more have appreciated one of Milton's or Shakespeare's smallest poems than she could have laughed over a page of Chinese. She liked to hear this and that popular preacher, and when her husband called his sermons humbug, she heard it with a shocked countenance; but was she better or worse than her husband when, admiring them as she did, she permitted them to have no more influence upon her conduct than if they had been the merest humbug ever uttered by ambitious demagogue? In truth, I cannot see that in the matter of worth there was much as yet to choose between them.

It is hardly necessary, then, to say that there was little appreciable approximation of any kind going on between them. If only they would have read Dickens together! Who knows what might have come of it! But this dull close animal proximity, without the smallest conscious nearness of heart or mind or soul—and so little chance, from very lack of wants, for showing each other kindnesses—surely it is a killing sort of thing! And yet, and yet, there is always a something—call it habit, or any poorest name you please—grows up between two who are much together, at least when they neither quarrel nor thwart each other's designs, which, tending with its roots towards the deeper human, blossoms into a wretched little flower indeed, yet afar off partaking of the nature of love. The Something seldom reveals its existence until they are parted. I suspect that with not a few, Death is the love-messenger at the stroke of whose dart the stream of love first begins to flow in the selfish bosom.

It is now necessary to mention a little break in the monotony of Mrs. Dempster's life, which, but for what came afterwards, could claim no record. One morning her page announced Major Strong, and possibly she received the gentleman who entered with a brighter face than she had ever shown her husband. The major had just arrived from India. He had been much at her father's house while she was yet a mere girl, being then engaged to one of her sisters, who died after he went abroad, and before he could return to marry her. He was now a widower, a fine-looking, frank, manly fellow. The expression of his countenance was little altered, and the sight of him revived in the memory of Mrs. Dempster many recollections of a happy girlhood, when the prospect of such a life as she now led with tolerable content would have seemed simply unendurable. When her husband came home she told him as much as he cared to hear of the visitor she had had, and he made no objection to her asking him to dine the next Sunday. When he arrived, Mr. Dempster saw a man of his own age, bronzed and big, with not much waist left, but a good carriage and pleasant face. He made himself agreeable at dinner, appreciated his host's wine, and told good stories that pleased the business man as showing that he knew "what was what." He accorded him his more particular approval, speaking to his wife, on the ground that he was a man of the world, with none of the army slang about him. Mr. Dempster was not aware that he had himself more business peculiarities than any officer in her majesty's service had military ones.

After this Major Strong frequently called upon Mrs. Dempster. They were good friends, and did each other no harm whatever, and the husband neither showed nor felt the least jealousy. They sang together, occasionally went out shopping, and three or four times went together to the play. Mr. Dempster, so long as he had his usual comforts, did not pine in his wife's absence, but did show a little more pleasure when she came home to him than usually when he came home to her. This lasted for a few months. Then the major went back to India, and for a time the lady missed him a good deal, which, considering the dulness of her life, was not very surprising or reprehensible.

II: AN ASTONISHMENT

NOW comes the strange part of my story.

One evening the housemaid opened the door to Mr. Dempster on his return from the city; and perhaps the fact that it was the maid, and not the page as usual, roused his observation, which, except in business matters, was not remarkably operative. He glanced at the young woman, when an eye far less keen than his could not have failed to remark a strangely excited expression on her countenance.

"Where is the boy?" he asked.

"Just run to the doctor's, sir," she answered.

Then first he remembered that when he left in the morning his wife had not been feeling altogether well, but he had never thought of her since.

"How is your mistress?" he said.

"She's rather poorly, sir, but—but—she's as well as could be expected."

"What does the fool mean?" said Dempster to himself, and very nearly said it aloud, for he was not over polite to any in his service. But he did not say it aloud. He advanced into the hall with deliberation, and made for the stair.

"Oh, please, sir," the maid cried in a tone of perturbation, when, turning from shutting the door, she saw his intention, "you can't go up to mis'ess's room just at this minute, sir. Please go in the dining-room, sir."

"What do you mean?" he asked, turning angrily upon the girl, for of all things he hated mystery.

Like every one else in the house, and office both, she stood in awe of him, and his look frightened her.

"Please go in the dining-room," she gasped entreatingly.

"What!" he said and did turn towards the dining-room, "is your mistress so ill she can't see me?"

"Oh, no, sir!—at least I don't know exactly. Cook's with her, sir. She's over the worst, anyhow."

"What on earth do you mean girl? Speak out, will you? What is the matter with your mistress?"

As he spoke he stepped into the room, the maid following him. The same moment he spied a whitish bundle of something on the rug in front of the fire.

"What do you mean by leaving things like that in the dining-room?" he went on more angrily still.

"Please, sir," answered the girl, going and lifting the bundle carefully, "it's the baby!"

"The baby!" shouted Mr. Dempster, and looked at her from head to foot. "What baby?" Then bethinking himself that it must belong to some visitor in the drawing-room with his wife, he moderated his tone. "Make haste; take it away!" he said. "I don't want babies here! There's a time and a place for everything!—What *are* you about?"

For, instead of obeying her master and taking it away, the maid was carefully looking in the blanket for the baby. Having found it and turned aside the covering from its face, she came nearer, and holding up the little vision, about the size and colour of a roll of red wax taper, said:—

"Look at it, sir! It's your own, and worth looking at."

Never before had she dared speak to him so!

I will not venture to assert that Mr. Dempster turned white, but his countenance changed, and he dropped into the chair behind him, feeling less of a business man than had been his consciousness for the last twenty hears. He was hit hard. The absolutely Incredible had hit him. Babies might be born

147

in a day, but surely not without previous preparation on the part of Nature at least, if not on that of the mother; and in this case if the mother had prepared herself, certainly she had not prepared him for the event. It was as if the treasure of Nature's germens were tumbling all together. His head swam. He could not speak a word.

"Yes, sir," the maid went on, relieved of her trepidation in perceiving that her master too was mortal, and that her word had such power over him—proud also of knowing more of his concerns than he did himself, "she was took about an hour and a half ago. We've kep' sendin' and' sendin' after the doctor, but he ain't never been yet; only cook, she knows a deal an' she says she's been very bad, sir. But the young gentleman come at last, bless him! and now she's doin' as well as could be expected, sir—cook say."

"God bless me!" said the astonished father, and relapsed into the silence of bewilderment.

Eight years married with never a glimmer of offspring—and now, all at once, and without a whisper of warning, the father of a "young gentleman!" How could it be other than perplexing—discomposing, indeed—yet it was right pleasant too. Only it would have been more pleasant if experience could have justified the affair! Nature—no, not Nature—or, if Nature, then Nature sure in some unnatural mood, had stolen a march upon him, had gone contrary to all that had ever been revealed of her doings before! and why had she pitched on him—just him, Duncan Dempster, to exercise one of her more grotesque and wayward moods upon?—to play at hide-and-seek with after this fashion? She had not treated him with exactly proper respect, he thought, or, rather vaguely felt.

"Business is business," he remarked, under his breath, "and this cannot be called proper business behaviour. What is there about me to make game of? Really, my wife ought—— "

What his wife ought or ought not to have done, however, had not yet made itself clear to him, and his endeavour to excogitate being in that direction broken off, gave way to the pleasure of knowing himself a father, or perhaps more truly of having an heir. In the strength of it he rose, went to the cellaret, and poured himself out a glass of his favourite port, which he sat down to drink in silence and meditation. He was rather a picture just then and there, though not a very lovely one, seated, with his hat still on his head, in the middle of the room, upon a chair half-way between the dining-table and the sideboard, with his glass of wine in his hand. He was pondering partly the pleasure, but still mainly the peculiarity of his position. A bishop once told me that, shortly after he had been raised to the episcopal dignity, a friend's horses, whose driver had tumbled off the box drunk, ran away with him, and upset the carriage. He crept out of the window over his head, and the first thought that came to him as he sat perched on the side of the carriage, while it was jumbled along by the maddened horses, was, "What do bishops do in such circumstances?" Equally perplexing was the question Dempster had to ask himself: how husbands who, after being married eight years, suddenly and unexpectedly received the gift of a first-born, were in the habit of comporting themselves! He poured himself out another glass, and with it came the reflection, both amusing and consoling, that his brother, who was confidently expecting his tidy five figures to crown the early bliss of one or more of his large family some day, would be equally but less agreeably surprised. "Serve him right!" he said to himself, "What business have they to be looking out for my death?" And for a moment the heavens appeared a little more just than he was ordinarily in the habit of regarding them. He said to himself he would work harder than ever now. There would now be some good in making money! He had never given his mind to it yet, he said: now the world should see what he could do when he did give his mind to it!

Hitherto gathering had been his main pleasure, but with the thought of his money would now not seldom be mingled the thought of the little thing in the blanket! He began to find himself strangely happy. I use the wrong phrase—for the fact is, he had never yet found himself at all; he knew nothing of the person except a self-painted and immensely flattered portrait that hung in the innermost chamber of his heart—I mean the innermost chamber he knew anything of: there were many chambers there of which he did not even know the doors. Yet a few minutes as he sat there, and he was actually cherishing a little pride in the wife who had done so much better for him than he had at length come to expect. If not a good accountant, she was at least a good wife, and a very fair housekeeper: he had no doubt she would prove a good mother. He would gladly have gone to her at once, to let her know how much he was pleased with her behaviour. As for that little bit of red clay— "terra cotta," he called it to himself, as he looked round with a smile at the blanket, which the housemaid had replaced on the rug before the fire—who could imagine him a potentate upon 'Change—perhaps in time a director of European affairs! He was not in the way of joking—of all things about money; the very thought of business filled him from top to toe with seriousness; but he did make that small joke, and accompany it with a grim smile.

He was startled from his musing by the entrance of the doctor, who had in the meantime arrived and seen the lady, and now came to look at the baby. He congratulated Mr. Dempster on having at length a son and heir, but warned him that his wife was far from being beyond danger yet. The whole thing was entirely out of the common, he said, and she must be taken the greatest possible care of. The words woke a gentle pity in the heart of the man, for by nature all men have some tenderness for women in such circumstances, but they did not trouble him greatly—for such dangers belonged to their calling, their *business* in life, and, doubtless, if she had attended to that business earlier she would have found it easier.

"Did you ever know such a thing before, doctor?" he asked, with the importance of one honoured by a personal visit from the Marvellous.

"Never in my own practice," answered the doctor, whom the cook had instructed in the wonders of the case, "but I have read of such a thing." And Mr. Dempster swelled like a turkey-cock.

It was several days before he was allowed to see the mother. Perhaps had she expressed a strong desire to see him, it might have been risked sooner, but she had neither expressed nor manifested any. He kissed her, spoke a few stupid words in a kind tone, asking her how she did, but paying no heed to her answer, and turned aside to look at the baby.

Mrs. Dempster recovered but slowly, and not very satisfactorily. She did not seem to care much about the child. She tried to nurse him, but was not very successful. She took him when the nurse brought him, and yielded him again with the same indifference, showing neither pleasure to receive nor unwillingness to part with him. The nurse did not fail to observe it and remark upon it: *she* had never seen a mother care so little for her child! There was little of the mother in *her* anyway! It was no wonder she was so long about it. It troubled the father a little that she should not care for his child: some slight fermentation had commenced in the seemingly dead mass of human affection that had lain so long neglected in his being, and it seemed strange to him that, while he was living for the child in the City, she should be so indifferent to him at home. For already he had begun to keep his vow, already his greater keenness in business was remarked in the City. But it boded little good for either that the gift of God should stir up in him the worship of Mammon. More sons are damned by their fathers' money than by anything else whatever outside of themselves.

There was the excuse to be made for Mrs. Dempster that she continued far from strong—and her husband made it: he would have made it more heartily if he had himself ever in his life known what it was to be ill. By degrees she grew stronger, however, until, to persons who had not known her before, she would have seemed in tolerable health. For a week or two after she was again going about the house, she continued to nurse the baby, but after that she became unable to do so, and therewith began to neglect him entirely. She never asked to see him, and when the nurse brought him would turn her head aside, and tell her to take it away. So far from his being a pleasure to her, the very sight of the child brought the hot dew upon her forehead. Her husband frowned and wondered, but, unaccustomed to open his mind either to her or to any one else, not unwisely sought to understand the thing before speaking of it, and in the meantime commenced a genuine attempt to make up to the baby for his mother's neglect. Almost without a notion how even to take him in his arms, he would now send for him the moment he had had his tea, and after a fashion, ludicrous in the eyes of the nurse, would dandle and caress him, and strut about with him before his wife, glancing up at her every now and then, to point the lesson that such was the manner in which a parent ought to behave to a child. In his presence she never made any active show of her dislike, but her look seemed all the time fixed on something far away, as if she had nothing to do with the affair.

III: ANOTHER ASTONISHMENT

BUT a second and very different astonishment awaited Mr. Dempster. Again one evening, on his return from the City, he saw a strange look on the face of the girl who opened the door—but this time it was a look of fear.

"Well?" he said, in a tone at once alarmed and peremptory.

She made no answer, but turned whiter than before.

"Where is your mistress?" he demanded.

"Nobody knows, sir," she answered.

"Nobody knows! What would you have me understand by such an answer?"

"It's the bare truth, sir. Nobody knows where she is."

"God bless me!" cried the husband. "What does it all mean?"

And again he sunk down upon a chair—this time in the hall, and stared at the girl as if waiting further enlightenment.

But there was little enough to be had. Only one point was clear: his wife was nowhere to be found. He sent for every one in the house, and cross-questioned each to discover the last occasion on which she had been seen. It was some time since she had been missed; how long before that she had been seen there was no certainty to be had. He ran to the doctor, then from one to another of her acquaintance, then to her mother, who lived on the opposite side of

London. She, like the rest, could tell him nothing. In her anxiety she would have gone back with him, but he was surly, and would not allow her. It was getting towards morning before he reached home, but no relieving news awaited him. What to think was as much a perplexity to him as what to do. He was not in the agony in which a man would have been who thoroughly loved his wife, but he cared enough about her to feel uncomfortable; and the cries of the child, who was suffering from some ailment, made him miserable: in his perplexity and dull sense of helplessness he wondered whether she might not have given the baby poison before she went. Then the thing would make such a talk! and, of all things, Duncan Dempster hated being talked about. How busy people's brains would be with all his affairs! How many explanations of the mystery would be suggested on 'Change! Some would say, "What business had a man like him with a fine lady for a wife? one so much younger than himself too!" He could remember making some remark of another, before he was married. "Served him right!" they would say. And with that the first movement of suspicion awoke in him—purely and solely from his own mind's reflection of the imagined minds of others. While in his mind's ear he heard them talking, almost before he knew what they meant the words came to him: "There was that Major Strong, you know!"

"She's gone to him!" he cried aloud, and, springing from the bed on which he had thrown himself, he paced the chamber in a fury. He had no word for it but hers that he was now in India! They had only been waiting till—by heaven, that child was none of his! And therewith rushed into his mind the conviction that everything was thus explained. No man ever yet entertained an unhappy suspicion, but straightway an army of proofs positive came crowding to the service of the lie. It is astounding with what manifest probability everything will fall in to prove that a fact which has no foundation whatever! There is no end to the perfection with which a man may fool himself while taking absolute precautions against being fooled by others. Every face, being a living fact, has endless sides and relations; but of all these, the man whose being hangs upon one thought, will see only those sides and relations which fall in with that thought. Dempster even recalled the words of the maid, "It's mis'ess's," as embodying the girl's belief that it was not master's. Where a man, whether by nature jealous or not, is in a jealous condition, there is no need of an Iago to parade before him the proofs of his wrong. It was because Shakespeare would neither have Desdemona less than perfect, nor Othello other than the most trusting and least suspicious of men, that he had to invent an all but incredible villain to effect the needful catastrophe.

But why should a man, who has cared so little for his wife, become instantly, upon the bare suspicion, so utter a prey to consuming misery? There was a character in his suffering which could not be attributed to any degree of anger, shame, or dread of ridicule. The truth was, there lay in his being a possibility of love to his wife far beyond anything his miserably stunted consciousness had an idea of; and the conviction of her faithlessness now wrought upon him in the office of Death, to let him know what he had lost. It magnified her beauty in his eyes, her gentleness, her grace; and he thought with a pang how little he had made of her or it.

But the next moment wrath at the idea of another man's child being imposed upon him as his, with the consequent loss of his precious money, swept every other feeling before it. For by law the child was his, whoever might be the father of it. During a whole minute he felt on the point of tying a stone about its neck, carrying it out, and throwing it into the river Lea. Then, with the laugh of a hyena, he set about arranging in his mind the proofs of her guilt. First came eight childless years with himself; next the concealment of her condition, and the absurd pretence that she had known nothing of it; then the trouble of mind into which she had fallen; then her strange unnatural aversion to her own child; and now, last of all, conclusive of a guilty conscience, her flight from his house. He would give himself no trouble to find her; why should he search after his own shame! He would neither attempt to conceal nor to explain the fact that she had left him—people might say what they pleased—try him for murder if they liked! As to the child she had so kindly left to console him for her absence, he would not drown him, neither would he bring him up in his house; he would give him an ordinary education, and apprentice him to a trade. For his money, he would leave it to a hospital—a rich one, able to defend his will if disputed. For what was the child? A monster—a creature that had no right to existence!

Not one of those who knew him best would have believed him capable of being so moved, nor did one of them now know it, for he hid his suffering with the success of a man not unaccustomed to make a mask of his face. There are not a few men who, except something of the nature of a catastrophe befall them, will pass through life without having or affording a suspicion of what is in them. Everything hitherto had tended to suppress the live elements of Duncan Dempster; but now, like the fire of a volcano in a land of ice, the vitality in him had begun to show itself.

Sheer weariness drove him, as the morning began to break, to lie down again; but he neither undressed nor slept, and rose at his usual hour. When he entered the dining-room, where breakfast was laid as usual—only for one instead of two—he found by his plate, among letters addressed to his wife, a packet directed to himself. It had not been through the post, and the address was in his wife's hand. He opened it. A sheet of paper was wrapped around a roll of unpaid butcher's bills, amounting to something like eighty pounds, and a note from the butcher craving immediate settlement. On the sheet of paper was written, also in his wife's hand, these words: "I am quite unworthy of being your wife any longer"; that was all.

Now here, to a man who had loved her enough to understand her, was a clue to the whole—to Dempster it was the strongest possible confirmation of what he had already concluded. To him it appeared as certain as anything he called truth, that for years, while keeping a fair face to her husband—a man who had never refused her anything—he did not recall the fact that almost never had she asked or he offered anything—she had been deceiving him, spending money she would not account for, pretending to pay everything when she had been ruining his credit with the neighbourhood, making him, a far richer man than any but himself knew, appear to be living beyond his means, when he was every month investing far more than he spent. It was injury upon injury! Then, as a last mark of her contempt, she had taken pains that these beggarly butcher's bills should reach him from her own hand! He would trouble himself about such a woman not a moment longer!

He went from breakfast to his omnibus as usual, walked straight to his office, and spent the day according to custom. I need hardly say that the first thing he did was to write a cheque for the butcher. He made no further inquiry after her whatever, nor was any made of him there, for scarcely one of the people with whom he did business had been to his house, or had even seen his wife.

In the suburb where he lived it was different; but he paid no heed to any inquiry, beyond saying he knew nothing about her. To her relatives he said that if they wanted her they might find her for themselves. She had gone to please herself, and he was not going to ruin himself by running about the world after her.

Night after night he came home to his desolate house; took no comfort from his child; made no confession that he stood in need of comfort. But he had a dull sensation as if the sun had forsaken the world, and an endless night had begun. The simile, of course, is mine—the sensation only was his; *he* could never have expressed anything that went on in the region wherein men suffer.

A few days made a marked difference in his appearance. He was a hard man; but not so hard as people had thought him; and besides, *no* man can rule his own spirit except he has the spirit of right on his side; neither is any man proof against the inroads of good. Even Lady Macbeth was defeated by the imagination she had braved. Add to this, that no man can, even by those who understand him best, be labelled as a box containing such and such elements, for the humanity in him is deeper than any individuality, and may manifest itself as some crisis in a way altogether beside expectation.

His feeling was not at first of an elevated kind. After the grinding wrath had abated, self-pity came largely to the surface—not by any means a grand emotion, though very dear to boys and girls in their first consciousness of self, and in them pardonable enough. On the same ground it must be pardoned in a man who, with all his experience of the world, was more ignorant of the region of emotion, and more undeveloped morally, than multitudes of children: in

him it was an indication that the shell was beginning
to break. He said to himself that he was old beside
her, and that she had begun to weary of him, and
despise him. Gradually upon this, however, super-
vened at intervals a faint shadow of pity for her who
could not have been happy or she would not have left
him.

Days and weeks passed, and there was no sign of
Mrs. Dempster. The child was not sent out to nurse,
and throve well enough. His father never took the
least notice of him.

IV: WHAT IT MEANT

SOME of my readers, perhaps all of them, will have
concluded that Mrs. Dempster was a little out of
her mind. Such, indeed, was the fact, and one not
greatly to be wondered at, after such a peculiar experience as she had had. Some small degree of
congestion, and the consequent pressure on some
portion of the brain, had sent certain faculties to sleep,
and, perhaps, roused others into morbid activity. That
it is impossible to tell where sanity ends and insanity
begins, is a trite remark indeed; but like many things
which it is useless to say, it has the more need to be
thought of. If I yield to an impulse of which I know
I shall be ashamed, is it not the act of a madman?
And may not the act lead to a habit, and at length to
a despised, perhaps feared and hated, old age, twist-
ing at the ragged ends of a miserable life?

However certain it is that mental disorder had to
do with Mrs. Dempster's departure from her home,
it is almost as certain she would never have gone had
it not been for the unpaid bills haunting her consciousness, a combination of demon and ghost. The
misery had all the time been growing upon her, and
must have had no small share in the subversion of

her microcosm. When that was effected, the evil thing that lay at the root of it all rose and pounced upon her. Wrong is its own avenger. She had been doing wrong, and knowingly for years, and now the plant of evil was blossoming towards its fruit. If one say the evil was but a trifle, I take her judgment, not his, upon that. She had been lazy towards duty, had persistently turned aside from what she knew to be her business, until she dared not even look at it. And now that the crisis was at hand, as omened by that letter from the butcher, with the sense of her wrongdoing was mingled the terror of her husband. What would he think, say, and do? Not yet had she, after all these years, any deep insight into his character; else perhaps she might have read there that, much as he loved money, the pleasure of seeing signal failure follow the neglect of his instructions would quite compensate him for the loss. What the bills amounted to, she had not an idea. Not until she had made up her mind to leave her home could she muster the courage to get them together. Then she even counted up the total and set down the sum in her memory— which sum thereafter haunted her like the name of her devil.

As to the making up of her mind—she could remember very little of that process—or indeed of the turning of her resolve into action. She left the house in the plainest dress her wardrobe could afford her, and with just one half-crown in her pocket. Her design was to seek a situation, as a refuge from her husband and his wrath. It was a curious thing, that, while it gave her no trouble to leave her baby, whom indeed she had not that day seen, and to whom for some time she had ceased to be necessary, her only notion was to get a place as nurse.

At that time, I presume, there were few or no such offices for engaging servants as are now common; at all events, the plan Mrs. Dempster took, when she had reached a part of London she judged sufficiently distant for her purpose, was to go from shop to shop inquiring after a situation. But she met with no prospect of success, and at last, greatly in need of rest and refreshment, went into a small coffee shop. The woman who kept it was taken by her appearance, her manners, and her evident trouble, and, happening to have heard of a lady who wanted a nurse, gave her the address. She went at once, and applied for the place. The lady was much pleased with her, and agreed to take her, provided she received a satisfactory character of her. For such a demand Mrs. Dempster was unprepared; she had never thought what reference she could give, and, her resources for deception easily exhausted, gave, driven to extremity, the name and address of her mother. So met the extremes of loss and salvation! She returned to the coffee shop, and the lady wrote at once to the address of the young woman's late mistress, as she supposed.

The kindness of her new friend was not exhausted; she gave her a share of her own bed that night. Mrs. Dempster had now but two shillings, which she offered her, promising to pay her the rest out of the first wages she received. But the good woman would take no more than one of them, and that in full payment of what she owed her, and Mrs. Dempster left the shop in tears, to linger about the neighbourhood until the hour should arrive at which the lady had told her to call again. Apparently she must have cherished the hope that her mother, divining her extremity, would give her the character she could honestly claim. But as she drew near the door which she hoped would prove a refuge, her mother was approaching it also, and at the turning of a corner they ran into each other's arms. The elderly lady had a hackney coach waiting for her in the next street, and Mrs. Dempster, too tired to resist, got into it at once at her mother's desire. Ere they reached the mother's house, which, as I have said, was a long way from Mr. Dempster's, the daughter told everything, and the mother had perceived more than the daughter could tell: her eyes had revealed that all was not right behind them. She soothed her as none but a mother can, easily persuading her she would make everything right, and undertaking herself to pay the money owing to the butcher. But it was soon evident that for the present there must be no suggestion of her going back to her husband; for, imagining from something, that her mother was taking her to him, she jumped up and had all but opened the door of the cab when her mother succeeded in mastering her. As soon as she was persuaded that such had never been the intention, she was quiet. When they reached the house, she was easily induced to go to bed at once.

Her mother lived in a very humble way, with one servant, a trustworthy woman. To her she confided the whole story, and with her consulted as to what had better be done. Between them they resolved to keep her, for a while at least, in retirement and silence. To this conclusion they came on the following grounds: First, the daughter's terror and the mother's own fear of Mr. Dempster; next, it must be confessed, the resentment of both mistress and servant because of his rudeness when he came to inquire after her; third, the evident condition of the poor creature's mind; and last, the longing of the two women to have her to themselves, that they might nurse and cosset her to their hearts' content.

They were to have more of this indulgence, however, than, for her sake, they would have desired, for before morning she was very ill. She had brain fever, in fact, and they had their hands full, especially as they desired to take every precaution to prevent the neighbourhood from knowing there was any one but themselves in the house.

It was a servere attack, but she passed the crisis favourably, and began to recover. One morning, after a quieter night than usual, she called her mother, and told her she had had a strange dream—that she had a baby somewhere, but could not find him, and was wandering about looking for him.

"Wasn't it a curious dream, mamma?" she said. "I wish it were a true one. I knew exactly what my baby was like, and went into house after house full of children, sure that I could pick him out of thousands. I was just going up to the door of the Foundling Hospital to look for him there when I woke."

As she ceased, a strange trouble passed like a cloud over her forehead and eyes, and her hand, worn almost transparent by the fever, followed it over forehead and eyes. She seemed trying to recall something forgotten. But her mother thought it better to say nothing.

Each of the two nights following she had the same dream.

"Three times, mother," she said. "I am not superstitious, as you know, but I can't help feeling as if it must mean something. I don't know what to make of it else—except it be that I haven't got over the fever yet. And, indeed, I am afraid my head is not quite right, for I can't be sure sometimes, such a hold has my dream of me, that I haven't got a baby somewhere about the world. Give me your hand, mother, and sing to me."

Still her mother thought it more prudent to say nothing, and do what she could to divert her thoughts; for she judged it must be better to let her brain come right, as it were, of itself.

In the middle of the next night she woke her with a cry.

"O, mother, mother! I know it all now. I am not out of my mind any more. How I came here I cannot tell—but I know I have a husband and a baby at Hackney—and—oh, such a horrible roll of butcher's bills!"

"Yes, yes, my dear! I know all about it," answered her mother. "But never mind; you can pay them all yourself now, for I heard only yesterday that your Aunt Lucy is dead, and has left you the hundred pounds she promised you twenty years ago."

"Oh, bless her!" cried Mrs. Dempster, springing out of bed, much to the dismay of her mother, who boded a return of the fever. "I must go home to my baby at once. But tell me about it, mamma. How did I come here? I seem to remember being in a carriage with you, and that is the last I know."

Then, upon condition that she got into bed at once, and promised not to move until she gave her leave, her mother consented to tell her all she knew. She listened in silence, with face flushed and eyes glowing, but drank a cooling draught, lay down again, and at daybreak was fast asleep. When she awoke she was herself again.

V: WHAT CAME OF IT

MEANTIME, things were going, as they should, in rather a dull fashion with Duncan Dempster. His chariot wheels were gone, and he drove heavily. The weather was good; he seldom failed of the box-seat on the omnibus; a ray of light, the first he had ever seen there, visited his table, reflected from a new window on the opposite side of a court into the heart of his dismal back office; and best of all, business was better than usual. Yet was Dempster not cheerful. He was not, indeed, a man an acquaintance would ever have thought of calling cheerful; but in grays there are gradations; and however differently a man's barometer may be set from those of other people, it has its ups and downs, its fair weather and foul. But not yet had he an idea how much his mental equilibrium had been dependent upon the dim consciousness of having that quiet uninterested wife in the comfortable house at Hackney. It had been stronger than it seemed, the spidery, invisible line connecting that office and that house, along which had run twice a day the hard dumpling that dwelt in Mr. Dempster's bosom. Vaguely connected with that home after all must have been that endless careful gathering of treasure in the city; for now, though he could no more stop making money than he could stop breathing, it had not the same interest as formerly. Indeed, he had less interest than before in keeping his lungs themselves going. But he kept on doing everything as usual.

Not one of the men he met ever said a word to him about his wife. The general impression was that she had left him for preferable society, and no one wondered at her throwing aside such "a dry old stick" whom even the devoted slaves of business contemned as having nothing in him but business.

A further change was, however, in progress within him. The first sign of it was that he began to doubt whether his wife had indeed been false to him—had forsaken him in any other company than that of Death. But there was not great difficulty in the way of the conclusion. It was impossible for him to imagine suicide as proceeding from any cause but insanity, and what could have produced the disorder in one who had no cares or anxieties, everything she wanted, and nothing to trouble her, a devoted husband, and a happy home? Yet the mere idea made him think more pitifully, and so more tenderly of her than before. It had not yet occurred to him to consider whether he might not have had something to do with her conduct or condition. Blame was a thing he had never made acquaintance with—least of all in the form of self-blame. To himself he was simply all right—the posed centre of things capable of righteous judgment on everyone else. But it must not be forgotten how little he knew about his own affairs at all; his was a very different condition from that of one who had closed his eyes and hardened his heart to suspicions concerning himself. His eyes had never yet been opened to anything but the order of things in the money world—its laws, its penalties, its rewards—those he did understand. But apparently he was worth troubling. A slow dissatisfaction was now preying upon him—a sense of want—of not having something he once had, a vague discomfort, growing restless. The feeling was no doubt the worse that the birth of the child had brought such a sudden rush of fresh interest into his occupation, which doubt concerning that birth had again so suddenly checked; but even if the child should prove after all his own, a supposition he was now willing to admit as possibly a true one, he could never without his mother feel any enthusiasm about him, even such enthusiasm as might be allowed to a man who knew money from moonshine, and common sense from hysterics. Yet once and again, about this time, the nurse coming into the room after a few minutes' absence, found him bending over the sleeping infant, and, as she described him, "looking as if he would have cried if he had only known how."

One frosty evening in late autumn the forsaken husband came from London—I doubt if he would now have said "home"—as usual, on the top of the omnibus. His was a tough nature physically, as well as morally, and if he had found himself inside an omnibus he would have thought he was going to die.

The sun was down. A green hue rose from the horizon half-way to the zenith, but a pale yellow lingered over the vanished sun, like the gold at the bottom of a chrysolite. The stars were twinkling small and sharp in the azure overhead. A cold wind blew in little gusts, now from this side, now from that, as they went steadily along. The horses' hoofs rang loud on the hard road. The night got hold of him: it was at this season, and on nights like these, that he had haunted the house of Lucy's father, doing his best to persuade her to make him, as he said, a happy man. It now seemed as if then, and then only, he had been a happy man. Certainly, of all his life, it was the time when he came nearest to having a peep out of the upper windows of the house of life. He had been a dweller in the lower regions, a hewer of wood to the god of the cellar; and after his marriage, he had gone straight down again to the temple of the earthy god—to a worship whose god and temple and treasure caves will one day drop suddenly from under the votary's feet, and leave him dangling in the air without even a pocket about him—without even his banker's book to show for his respectability.

The night, I say, recalled the lovely season of his courtship, and again, in the mirror of loss, he caught a glimpse of things beyond him. Ah, if only that time and its hopes had remained with him! How different things would have been now! If Lucy had proved what he thought her!—remained what she seemed—the gentle, complaisant, yielding lady he imagined her, promising him a life of bliss! Alas, she would not even keep account of five pounds a week to please him! He never thought whether he, on his part, might not have, in some measure, come short of her expectations in a husband; whether she, the more lovely in inward design and outward fashion, might not have indulged yet more exquisite dreams of bliss which,

by devotion to his ideal of life, he had done his part
in disappointing. He only thought what a foolishness
it all was; that thus it would go on to the end of the
book; that youth after youth would have his turn of
such a wooing, and such a disappointment. Sunsets,
indeed! The suns of man's happiness never did anything but set! Out of money even—and who could
say there was any poetry in that?—there was not half
the satisfaction to be got that one expected. It was all
a mess of expectations and disappointments mashed
up together—nothing more. That was the world—on
a fair judgment.

Such were his reflections till the driver pulled up
for him to get down at his own gate. As he got down
the said driver glanced up curiously at the row of
windows on the first floor, and as soon as Mrs.
Dempster's back was turned, pointed to them with
the butt-end of his whip, and nodded queerly to the
gentleman who sat on his other side.

"That's more'n I've seen this six weeks," he said.
"There's something more'n common up this evenin',
sir."

There was light in the drawing-room—that was all
the wonder, but at those windows Mr. Dempster himself looked so fixedly that he had nearly stumbled up
his own door-steps.

He carried a latch-key now, for he did not care to
stand at the door till the boy answered the bell; people's eyes, as they passed, seemed to burn holes in
the back of his coat.

He opened the street door quietly, and went straight
up the stair to the drawing-room. Perhaps he thought
to detect some liberty taken by his servants. He was
a little earlier than usual. He opened that door, took
two steps into the room, and stood arrested, motionless. With his shabby hat on his head, his shabby
greatcoat on his back—for he grudged every penny

spent on his clothes—his arms hanging down by his sides, and his knees bent, ready to tremble, he looked not a little out of keeping in the soft-lighted, dainty, delicate-hued drawing-room. Could he believe his eyes? The light of a large lamp was centred upon a gracious figure in white—his wife, just as he used to see her before he married her! That was the way her hair would break loose as she ran down the stair to meet him!—only then there was no baby in her lap for it to fall over like a torrent of unlighted water over a white stone! It was a lovely sight.

He had stood but a moment when she looked up and saw him. She started, but gave no cry louder than a little moan. Instantly she rose. Turning, she laid the baby on the sofa, and flitted to him like a wraith. Arrived where he stood yet motionless, she fell upon her knees and clasped his. He was far too bewildered now to ask himself what husbands did in such circumstances, and stood like a block.

"Husband! husband!" she cried, "forgive me." With one hand she hid her face, although it was bent to the ground, and with the other held up to him a bit of paper. He took it from the thin white fingers; it might explain something—help him out of this bewilderment, half nightmare, half heavenly vision. He opened it. Nothing but a hundred-pound note! The familiar sight of bank paper, however, seemed to restore his speech.

"What does this mean, Lucy? Upon my word! Permit me to say—— "

He was growing angry.

"It is to pay the butcher," she said, with a faltering voice.

"Damn the butcher!" he cried. "I hope you've got something else to say to me! Where have you been all this time?"

"At my mother's. I've had a brain fever, and been out of my mind. It was all about the butcher's bill."

Dempster stared. Perhaps he could not understand how a woman who would not keep accounts should be to such a degree troubled at the result of her neglect.

"Look at me, if you don't believe me," she cried, and as she spoke she rose and lifted her face to his.

He gazed at it for a moment—pale, thin, and worn; and out of if shone the beautiful eyes, larger than before, but shimmering uncertain like the stars of a humid night, although they looked straight into his.

Something queer was suddenly the matter with his throat—something he never felt before—a constriction such as, had he been superstitious, he might have taken for the prologue to a rope. Then the thought came—what a brute he must be that his wife should have been afraid to tell him her trouble! Thereupon he tried to speak, but his throat was irresponsive to his will. Eve's apple kept sliding up and down in it, and would not let the words out. He had never been so served by members of his own body in his life before! It was positive rebellion, and would get him into trouble with his wife. There it was! Didn't he say so?

"Can't you forgive me, Mr. Dempster?" she said, and the voice was so sweet and so sad! "It is my own money. Aunt Lucy is dead, and left it me. I think it will be enough to pay all my debts; and I promise you—I do promise you that I will set down every halfpenny after this. Do try me once again—for baby's sake."

This last was a sudden thought. She turned and ran to the sofa. Dempster stood where he was, fighting the strange uncomfortable feeling in his throat. It would not yield a jot. Was he going to die suddenly

He gazed at her face for a moment —
pale, thin, and worn;
and out of it shone the beautiful eyes.

of choking? Was it a judgment upon him? Diphtheria, perhaps! It was much about in the City!

She was back, and holding up to him their sleeping child.

The poor fellow was not half the brute he looked—only he could *not* tell what to do with that confounded lump in his throat! He dared not try to speak, for it only choked him the more. He put his arms round them both, and pressed them to his bosom. Then the lump in his throat melted and ran out at his eyes, and all doubt vanished like a mist before the sun. But he never knew that he had wept. His wife did, and that was enough.

The next morning, for the first time in his life, he lost the eight o'clock omnibus.

The following Monday morning she brought her week's account to him. He turned from it testily, but she insisted on his going over it. There was not the mistake of a halfpenny. He went to town with a smile in his heart, and that night brought her home a cheque for ten pounds instead of five.

One day, in the middle of the same week, he came upon her sitting over the little blue-and-red-ruled book with a troubled countenance. She took no notice of his entrance.

"Do leave those accounts," he said, "and attend to me."

She shook her head impatiently, and made him no other answer. One moment more, however, and she started up, threw her arms about his neck, and cried triumphantly,

"It's buttons!—fourpence-halfpenny I paid for buttons!"

BIRTH, DREAMING, DEATH
The Schoolmaster's Story

IN a little room, scantily furnished, lighted, not from the window, for it was dark without, and the shutters were closed, but from the peaked flame of a small, clear-burning lamp, sat a young man, with his back to the lamp and his face to the fire. No book or paper on the table indicated labour just forsaken; nor could one tell from his eyes, in which the light had all retreated inwards, whether his consciousness was absorbed in thought, or reverie only. The window curtains, which scarcely concealed the shutters, were of coarse texture, but of brilliant scarlet,—for he loved bright colours; and the faint reflection they threw on his pale, thin face, made it look more delicate than it would have seemed in pure daylight. Two or three bookshelves, suspended by cords from a nail in the wall, contained a collection of books, poverty-stricken as to numbers, with but few to fill up the chronological gap between the Greek New Testament and stray volumes of the poets of the present century. But his love for the souls of his individual books was the stronger that there was no possibility of its degenerating into avarice for the bodies or outsides whose

Reprinted from *Adela Cathcart* (1864).

aggregate constitutes the piece of house-furniture called a library.

"Some years before, the young man (my story is so short, and calls in so few personages, that I need not give him a name) had aspired, under the influence of religious and sympathetic feeling, to be a clergyman; but Providence, either in the form of poverty, or of theological difficulty, had prevented his prosecuting his studies to that end. And now he was *only* a village schoolmaster; but is it not better to be a teacher *of* babes than a preacher *to* men, at any time; not to speak of those troublous times of transition, wherein a difference of degree must so often assume the appearance of a difference of kind? That man is more happy—I will not say more blessed—who, loving boys and girls, is loved and revered by them, than he who, ministering unto men and women, is compelled to pour his words into the filter of religious suspicion, whence the water is allowed to pass away unheeded, and only the residuum is retained for the analysis of ignorant party-spirit.

"He had married a simple village girl, in whose eyes he was nobler than the noblest—to whom he was the mirror, in which the real forms of all things around were reflected. Who dares pity my poor village schoolmaster? I fling his pity away. Had he not found in her love the verdict of God, that he was worth loving? Did he not in her possess the eternal and the unchangeable? Were not her eyes openings through which he looked into the great depths that could not be measured or represented? She was his public, his society, his critic. He found in her the heaven of his rest. God gave unto him immortality, and he was glad. For his ambition, it had died of its own mortality. He read the words of Jesus, and the words of great prophets whom he has sent; and learned that the wind-tossed anemone is a word of God as real and true as the unbending oak beneath which it grows—that reality is an absolute existence precluding degrees. If his mind was, as his room, scantily furnished, it was yet lofty; if his light was small, it was brilliant. God lived, and he lived. Perhaps the highest moral height which a man can reach, and at the same time the most difficult of attainment, is the willingness to be *nothing* relatively, so that he attain that positive excellence which the original conditions of his being render not merely possible, but imperative. It is nothing to a man to be greater or less than another; to be esteemed or otherwise by the public or private world in which he moves. Does he, or does he not, behold and love and live the unchangeable, the essential, the divine? This he can only do according as God has made him. He can behold and understand God in the least degree, as well as in the greatest, only by the godlike within him; and he that loves thus the good and great has no room, no thought, no necessity for comparison and difference. The truth satisfies him. He lives in its absoluteness. God makes the glow-worm as well as the star; the light in both is divine. If mine be an earth-star to gladden the wayside, I must cultivate humbly and rejoicingly its green earth-glow, and not seek to blanch it to the whiteness of the stars that lie in the fields of blue. For to deny God in my own being is to cease to behold him in any. God and man can meet only by the man's becoming that which God meant him to be. Then he enters into the house of life, which is greater than the house of fame. It is better to be a child in a green field than a knight of many orders in a state ceremonial.

"All night long he had sat there, and morning was drawing nigh. He has not heard the busy wind all night, heaping up snow against the house, which will make him start at the ghostly face of the world when at length he opens the shutters, and it stares upon him so white. For up in a little room above, white-curtained, like the great earth without, there has been a storm, too, half the night—moanings and prayers—and some forbidden tears; but now, at length, it is over; and through the portals of two mouths instead of one, flows and ebbs the tide of the great air-sea which feeds the life of man. With the sorrow of the mother, the new life is purchased for the child; our very being is redeemed from nothingness with the pains of a death of which we know nothing.

"An hour has gone by since the watcher below has been delivered from the fear and doubt that held him. He has seen the mother and the child—the first she has given to life and him, and has returned to his lonely room, quiet and glad.

"But not long did he sit thus before thought of doubt awoke in his mind. He remembered his scanty income, and the somewhat feeble health of his wife. One of two small debts he had contracted seemed absolutely to press on his bosom; and the newborn child—'oh! how doubly welcome,' he thought, 'if I were but half as rich again as I am!'—brought with it, as its own love, so its own care. The dogs of need, that so often hunt us up to heaven, seemed hard upon his heels; and he prayed to God with fervour; and as he prayed he fell asleep in his chair, and as he slept he dreamed. The fire and the lamp burned on as before, but threw no rays into his soul; yet now, for the first time, he seemed to become aware of the storm without; for his dream was as follows:

"He lay in his bed, and listened to the howling of the wintry wind. He trembled at the thought of the pitiless cold, and turned to sleep again, when he thought he heard a feeble knocking at the door. He rose in haste, and went down with a light. As he opened the door, the wind, entering with a gust of frosty particles, blew out his candle; but he found it unnecessary, for the grey dawn had come. Looking out, he saw nothing at first; but a second look, turned downwards, showed him a little half-frozen child, who looked quietly, but beseechingly, in his face. His hair was filled with drifted snow, and his little hands and cheeks were blue with cold. The heart of the schoolmaster swelled to bursting with the spring-flood of love and pity that rose up within it. He lifted the child to his bosom, and carried him into the house, where, in the dream's incongruity, he found a fire blazing in the room in which he now slept. The child said never a word. He set him by the fire, and made haste to get hot water, and put him in a warm bath. He never doubted that this was a stray orphan who had wandered to him for protection, and he felt that he could not part with him again; even though the train of his previous troubles and doubts once more passed through the mind of the dreamer, and there seemed no answer to his perplexities for the lack of that cheap thing, gold—yea, silver. But when he had undressed and bathed the little orphan, and having dried him on his knees, set him down to reach something warm to wrap him in, the boy suddenly looked up in his face, as if revived, and said with a heavenly smile, 'I am the child Jesus.' 'The child Jesus!' said the dreamer, astonished. 'Thou art like any other child.' 'No, do not say so,' returned the boy; 'but say, *Any other child is like me.*' And the child and the dream slowly faded away; and he awoke with these words sounding in his heart—'Whosoever shall receive one of such children in my name, receiveth me; and whosoever shall receive me, receiveth not me, but him that sent me.' It was the voice of God saying to him; 'Thou wouldst receive the child whom I sent thee out of the cold, stormy night; receive the new child out of the cold waste into the warm, human house, as the door by which it can enter God's house, its home. If better could be done for it, or for thee, would I have sent it hither? Through thy love, my little one must learn my love and be blessed. And thou shalt not keep it without thy reward. For thy necessities—in thy little house, is there not yet room? in thy barrel, is there not yet meal? and thy purse is not empty quite. Thou canst not eat more than a mouthful at once. I have made thee so. Is it any trouble to me to take care of thee? Only I prefer to feed thee from my own hand, and not from thy store.' And the schoolmaster sprang up in joy, ran up stairs, kissed his wife, and clasped the baby in his arms in the name of the child Jesus. And in that embrace, he knew that he received God to his heart. Soon, with a tender, beaming face, he was wading through the snow to the school-house, where he spent a happy day amidst the rosy faces and bright eyes of his boys and girls. These, likewise, he loved the more dearly and joyfully for that dream, and those words in his heart; so that, amidst their true child-faces, (all going well with them, as not infrequently happened in his schoolroom), he felt as if all the elements of Paradise were gathered around him, and knew that he was God's child, doing God's work.

"But while that dream was passing through the soul of the husband, another visited the wife, as she lay in the faintness and trembling joy of the new motherhood. For although she that has been mother before, is not the less a new mother to the new child, her former relation not covering with its wings the fresh bird in the nest of her bosom, yet there must be a peculiar delight in the thoughts and feelings that come with the first-born.—As she lay half in a sleep, half in a faint, with the vapours of a gentle delirium floating through her brain, without losing the sense of existence she lost the consciousness of its form, and thought she lay, not a young mother in her bed, but a nosegay of wild flowers in a basket, crushed, flattened and half-withered. With her in the basket lay other bunches of flowers, whose odours, some rare as well as rich, revealed to her the sad contrast in which she was placed. Beside her lay a cluster of delicately curved, faintly tinged, tea-scented roses; while she was only blue hyacinth bells, pale prim-roses, amethyst anemones, closed blood-coloured daisies, purple violets, and one sweet-scented, pure white orchis. The basket lay on the counter of a well-known little shop in the village, waiting for pur-chasers. By and by her own husband entered the shop, and approached the basket to choose a nose-gay. 'Ah!' thought she, 'will he choose me? How dreadful if he should not, and I should be left lying here, while he takes another! But how should he choose me? They are all so beautiful; and even my scent is nearly gone. And he cannot know that it is I lying here. Alas! alas!' But as she thought thus, she felt his hand clasp her, heard the ransom-money fall, and felt that she was pressed to his face and lips, as he passed from the shop. He *had* chosen her; he *had* known her. She opened her eyes: her husband's kiss had awakened her. She did not speak, but looked up thankfully in his eyes, as if he had, in fact, like one of the old knights, delivered her from the transfor-mation of some evil magic, by the counter-enchant-ment of a kiss, and restored her from a half-withered nosegay to be a woman, a wife, a mother. The dream comforted her much, for she had often feared that she, the simple, so-called uneducated girl, could not be enough for the great schoolmaster. But soon her thoughts flowed into another channel; the tears rose in her dark eyes, shining clear from beneath a stream that was not of sorrow; and it was only weakness that kept her from uttering audible words like these: —'Father in heaven, shall I trust my husband's love, and doubt thine? Wilt thou meet less richly the fearing hope of thy child's heart, than he in my dream met the longing of his wife's? He was perfected in my eyes by the love he bore me—shall I find thee less complete? Here I lie on thy world, faint, and crushed, and withered; and my soul often seems as if it had lost all the odours that should float up in the sweet-smelling savour of thankfulness and love to thee. But thou hast only to take me, only to choose me, only to clasp me to thy bosom, and I shall be a beautiful singing angel, singing to God, and comforting my husband while I sing. Father, take me, possess me, fill me!'

"So she lay patiently waiting for the summer-time of restored strength that drew slowly nigh. With her husband and her child near her, in her soul, and God everywhere, there was for her no death, and no hurt. When she said to herself, 'How rich I am!' it was with the riches that pass not away—the riches of the Son of man; for in her treasures, the human and the divine were blended—were one.

"But there was a hard trial in store for them. They had learned to receive what the Father sent: they had now to learn that what he gave he gave eternally, after his own being—his own glory. For ere the mother awoke from her first sleep, the baby, like a frolicsome child-angel, that but tapped at his mother's window and fled,—the baby died; died while the mother slept away the pangs of its birth; died while the father was teaching other babes out of the joy of his new fatherhood.

"When the mother woke, she lay still in her joy—the joy of a doubled life; and knew not that death had been there, and had left behind only the little human coffin.

" 'Nurse, bring me the baby,' she said at last. 'I want to see it.'

"But the nurse pretended not to hear.

" 'I want to nurse it. Bring it.'

"She had not yet learned to say *him*; for it was her first baby.

"But the nurse went out of the room, and remained some minutes away. When she returned, the mother spoke more absolutely, and the nurse was compelled to reply—at last.

" 'Nurse, do bring me the baby; I am quite able to nurse it now.'

" 'Not yet, if you please, ma'am. Really you must rest a while first. Do try to go to sleep.'

"The nurse spoke steadily, and looked her, too, straight in the face; and there was a constraint in her voice, a determination to be calm, that at once roused the suspicion of the mother; for though her first-born was dead, and she had given birth to what was now, as far as the eye could reach, the waxen image of a son, a child had come from God, and had departed to him again; and she *was* his mother.

"And the fear fell upon her heart that it might be as it was; and, looking at her attendant with a face blanched yet more with fear than with suffering, she said,

" 'Nurse, is the baby—— ?'

"She could not say *dead*; for to utter the word would be at once to make it possible that the only fruit of her labour had been pain and sorrow.

"But the nurse saw that further concealment was impossible; and, without another word, went and fetched the husband, who, with face pale as the mother's, brought the baby, dressed in its white clothes, and laid it by its mother's side, where it lay too still.

" 'Oh, ma'am, do not take on so,' said the nurse, as she saw the face of the mother grow like the face of the child, as if she were about to rush after him into the dark.

"But she was not 'taking on' at all. She only felt that pain at her heart, which is the farewell kiss of a long-cherished joy. Though cast out of paradise into a world that looked very dull and weary, yet, used to suffering, and always claiming from God the consolation it needed, and satisfied with that, she was able, presently, to look up in her husband's face, and try to reassure him of her well-being by a dreary smile.

" 'Leave the baby,' she said; and they left it where it was. Long and earnestly she gazed on the perfect tiny features of the little alabaster countenance, and tried to feel that this was the child she had been so long waiting for. As she looked, she fancied she heard it breathe, and she thought—'What if it should be only asleep!' but, alas! the eyes would not open, and when she drew it close to her, she shivered to feel it so cold. At length, as her eyes wandered over and over the little face, a look of her husband dawned unexpectedly upon it; and, as if the wife's heart awoke the mother's, she cried out, 'Baby! baby!' and burst into tears, during which weeping she fell asleep.

"When she awoke, she found the babe had been removed while she slept. But the unsatisfied heart of the mother longed to look again on the form of the child; and again, though with remonstrance from the nurse, it was laid beside her. All day and all night long, it remained by her side, like a little frozen thing that had wandered from its home, and now lay dead by the door.

"Next morning the nurse protested that she must part with it, for it made her fret; but she knew it quieted her, and she would rather keep her little lifeless babe. At length the nurse appealed to the father; and the mother feared he would think it necessary to remove it; but to her joy and gratitude he said, 'No, no; let her keep it as long as she likes.' And she loved her husband the more for that; for he understood her.

"Then she had the cradle brought near the bed, all ready as it was for a live child that had open eyes, and therefore needed sleep—needed the lids of the brain to close, when it was filled full of the strange colours and forms of the new world. But this one needed no cradle, for it slept on. It needed, instead of the little curtains to darken it to sleep, a great sunlight to wake it up from the darkness, and the ever-satisfied rest. Yet she laid it in the cradle, which she had set near her, where she could see it, with the little hand and arm laid out on the white coverlet. If she could only keep it so! Could not something be done, if not to awake it, yet to turn it to stone, and let it remain so for ever? No; the body must go back to its mother, the earth, and the *form* which is immortal, being the thought of God, must go back to its Father—the Maker. And as it lay in the white cradle, a white coffin was being made for it. And the mother thought: 'I wonder which trees are growing coffins for my husband and me.'

"But ere the child, that had the prayer of Job in his grief, and had died from its mother's womb, was carried away to be buried, the mother prayed over it this prayer:—'O God, if thou wilt not let me be a mother, I have one refuge: I will go back and be a child: I will be thy child more than ever. My mother-heart will find relief in childhood towards its Father. For is it not the same nature that makes the true mother and the true child? Is it not the same thought blossoming upward and blossoming downward? So there is God the Father and God the Son. Thou wilt keep my little son for me. He has gone home to be nursed for me. And when I grow well, I will be more simple, and truthful, and joyful in thy sight. And now thou art taking away my child, my plaything from me.

183

But I think how pleased I should be, if I had a daughter, and she loved me so well that she only smiled when I took her plaything from her. Oh! I will not disappoint thee—thou shalt have thy joy. Here I am, do with me what thou wilt; I will only smile.'

"And how fared the heart of the father? At first, in the bitterness of his grief, he called the loss of his child a punishment for his doubt and unbelief; and the feeling of punishment made the stroke more keen, and the heart less willing to endure it. But better thoughts woke within him ere long.

"The old woman who swept out his schoolroom, came in the evening to inquire after the mistress, and to offer her condolences on the loss of the baby. She came likewise to tell the news, that a certain old man of little respectability had departed at last, unregretted by a single soul in the village but herself, who had been his nurse through the last tedious illness.

"The schoolmaster thought with himself:

" 'Can that soiled and withered leaf of a man, and my little snow-flake of a baby, have gone the same road? Will they meet by the way? Can they talk about the same thing—anything? They must part on the borders of the shining land, and they could hardly speak by the way.'

" 'He will live four-and-twenty hours, nurse,' the doctor had said.

" 'No, doctor; he will die to-night,' the nurse had replied; during which whispered dialogue, the patient had lain breathing quietly, for the last of suffering was nearly over.

He was at the close of an ill-spent life, not so much selfishly towards others as indulgently towards himself. He had failed of true joy by trying often and perseveringly to create a false one; and now, about to knock at the gate of the other world, he bore with him no burden of the good things of this; and one might be tempted to say of him, that it were better he had not been born. The great majestic mystery lay before him—but when would he see its majesty?

"He was dying thus, because he had tried to live as Nature said he should not live; and he had taken his own wages—for the law of the Maker is the necessity of his creature. His own children had forsaken him, for they were not perfect as their Father in heaven, who maketh his sun to shine on the evil and on the good. Instead of doubling their care as his need doubled, they had thought of the disgrace he brought on them, and not of the duty they owed him; and now, left to die alone for them, he was waited on by this hired nurse, who, familiar with death-beds, knew better than the doctor, knew that he could live only a few hours.

"Stooping to his ear, she had told him, as gently as she could,—for she thought she ought not to conceal it—that he must die that night. He had lain silent for a few moments; then had called her, and, with broken and failing voice, had said, 'Nurse, you are the only friend I have; give me one kiss before I die.' And the woman-heart had answered the prayer.

" 'And,' said the old woman, 'he put his arms round my neck, and gave me a long kiss, such a long kiss! and then he turned his face away, and never spoke again.'

"So, with the last unction of a woman's kiss, with this baptism for the dead, he had departed.

" 'Poor old man! he had not quite destroyed his heart yet,' thought the schoolmaster. 'Surely it was the child-nature that woke in him at the last, when the only thing left for his soul to desire, the only thing he could think of as a preparation for the dread something, was a kiss. Strange conjunction, yet simple and natural! Eternity—a kiss. Kiss me; for I am going to the Unknown!—Poor old man!' the schoolmaster went on in his thoughts, 'I hope my baby has met him, and put his tiny hand in the poor old shaking hand, and so led him across the borders into the shining land, and up to where Jesus sits, and said to the Lord: "Lord, forgive this old man, for he knew not what he did." And I trust the Lord has forgiven him.'

"And then the bereaved father fell on his knees, and cried out:

" 'Lord, thou has not punished me. Thou wouldst not punish for a passing thought of troubled unbelief, with which I strove. Lord, take my child and his mother and me, and do what thou wilt with us. I know thou givest not, to take again.'

"And ere the schoolmaster could call his Protestantism to his aid, he had ended his prayer with the cry:

" 'And O God! have mercy upon the poor old man, and lay not his sins to his charge.'

"For, though a woman's kiss may comfort a man to eternity, it is not all he needs. And the thought of his lost child had made the soul of the father compassionate."

He ceased, and we sat silent.